green

Here's what people are saying about
GREEN....

"Adventure, comedy, and even a dash of romance."
—The Bulletin of the Center for Children's Books,
Recommended

"A fun, fresh take on leprechaun lore." *—Booklist*

"A sweet and original exploration of growing up and being true to yourself." *—Kidsreads.com*

"A great one for middle-school lovers of fantasy."
—Charlotte's Library

"Laura's writing is witty, funny and definitely true to her thirteen-year-old character." *—My Pile of Books*

green

Laura Peyton Roberts

A YEARLING BOOK

This is a work of fiction. Names, characters, places, and incidents either are the product of the author's imagination or are used fictitiously. Any resemblance to actual persons, living or dead, events, or locales is entirely coincidental.

Text copyright © 2010 by Laura Peyton Roberts
Cover photograph copyright © 2010 by Krister Engstrom

All rights reserved. Published in the United States by Yearling, an imprint of Random House Children's Books, a division of Random House, Inc., New York. Originally published in hardcover in the United States by Delacorte Press, an imprint of Random House Children's Books, a division of Random House, Inc., New York, in 2010.

Yearling and the jumping horse design are registered trademarks of Random House, Inc.

Visit us on the Web! www.randomhouse.com/kids

Educators and librarians, for a variety of teaching tools, visit us at www.randomhouse.com/teachers

The Library of Congress has cataloged the hardcover edition of this work as follows:
Roberts, Laura Peyton.
Green / Laura Peyton Roberts.—1st ed.
p. cm.
Summary: Abducted by leprechauns on her thirteenth birthday, Lilybet Green learns that there is more to her family tree—and to her bond with her grandmother—than she ever imagined.
ISBN 978-0-385-73558-2 (trade) — ISBN 978-0-385-90543-5 (lib. bdg.) —
ISBN 978-0-375-89545-6 (ebook)
[1. Leprechauns—Fiction. 2. Grandmothers—Fiction.] I.Title.
PZ7.R5433Gr 2010
[Fic]—dc22
2008054241

ISBN 978-0-440-42235-8 (pbk.)

Printed in the United States of America

10 9 8 7 6 5 4 3 2

First Yearling Edition 2011

Random House Children's Books supports the First Amendment and celebrates the right to read.

Many thanks to Wendy Loggia,
Pamela Bobowicz, Colleen Fellingham,
Barbara Perris, Carrie Andrews, Marci Senders,
Laura Blake Peterson, and Dick Roberts for
their help here and along the way.

For Edie,
my lucky charm
for thirteen years

Prologue

Four or five things arrived for me on my thirteenth birthday. There was a Gap gift card from Gram and a bookstore one from Aunt Sarah. My cousin, Gennifer, sent a CD she'd burned. There might have been another card, too, but I don't remember right now.

What I remember is the package.

I found it lying beneath the mailbox on my front porch, a box the size of a brick, wrapped in shabby brown paper and enough wrinkled tape to make me think, *Psycho bomber. Anthrax. Some poor creature lacking opposable thumbs.*

No sender's name. No return address. Not even any postage.

I looked up and down our tree-lined street. The Douglases' demented Great Dane had escaped again and was tearing around Ms. Clark's front lawn despite her big rotating sprinkler. A dog and a sprinkler—those were the only things moving. Even the air was still.

Lifting the package off the porch, I sat with it on the bench by our front door. My name and address were printed on a scrap of paper attached to the front:

MISS LILYBET GREEN
1445 MARIGOLD COURT
PROVIDENCE, CALIFORNIA

I'm going to have to kill someone, I thought, squinting at the unfamiliar handwriting. Nobody in Providence—or any of the last three towns I'd lived in—even knew my real name. I'd been going by Lily for at least six years, ever since I'd figured out Lilybet was a guaranteed hard time for the new girl. Even my mother called me Lily now.

I thought about waiting for her to get home to watch me open my package. Then I started ripping.

After all, it was my birthday.

The explosion knocked me off the bench and broke our living room window. I remember the flash, the sting of gunpowder in my nose, the porch boards thumping the back of my head. The Douglases' dog started howling, but I could barely hear him over the ringing in my ears.

I remember lying on my back, staring up into the porch overhang, seeing the peeling paint there fade from white to gray to black.

I especially remember the black, all shot through with green sparks, like a sky full of fireworks, dancing green and red diamonds. Nearer. Then farther.

Then black.

Chapter 1

"She's like . . . terminally uncoordinated," Ainsley Williams said, loud enough to reach the whole class. I pretended not to hear, but tears stung my eyes as Ainsley's clique giggled. My crashes to the floor hurt less than their constant ridicule.

"You're all right, Lily. Walk it off," Ms. Carlson called, but even she sounded disgusted. Next to forward rolls and cartwheels, roundoffs were the easiest move we did, yet three weeks into summer gymnastics class, I still hadn't landed one. The only landing I'd mastered was on my butt.

Struggling to my feet, I limped off the rubbery blue mat

and tried to blend into the wall. Jayce Mason tumbled next, turning in a perfect roundoff and adding a back handspring to make me look even worse. The class was Beginning Gymnastics, but I was the only girl there who hadn't taken *any* gymnastics before. Worse, Ainsley, Jayce, and their group were all in ballet, too, so they knew how to move gracefully. I couldn't have fit in less.

"Nice leotard, you bug-eyed freak," Jayce taunted through her smile as she ran back past me to her friends.

Tears clogged my throat and I was afraid they might spill over. I didn't care what those girls thought—at least, I knew I shouldn't—but having no one on my side hurt. I never even had a good comeback. I cast a sideways glance at Martina Gregory, leaning against the wall a few feet away, but Marti's answering smile was slight and vague. She wasn't about to cross Team Ainsley by offering me any sympathy.

The rest of the girls threw their roundoffs without problems. The next tumbling pass was front walkovers. When my turn came, I stayed glued to the wall and waved Heather Giannini on past me. Another teacher might have called me out, but Ms. Carlson let it slide. I think we had both had enough.

"Okay," she said, clapping. "Split into apparatus groups for beam, bars, and vault. Except for anyone who would rather continue practicing on the floor." She looked in my direction. I hung my head and stayed where I was while all the other girls matched up with friends and ran off to use the equipment.

I had been on the outside all year here in Providence, ever since Mom had moved us again to take another promotion and transfer. We had already moved for her bank once before. I still didn't understand why she couldn't just get a better job where we already lived, but according to her, that attitude showed how little I knew about being a single working mother with only a high school education. What was obvious was that work was more important to her than whether I had any friends.

I dared to peek at the uneven bars. The bars were the most popular piece of equipment, so of course Ainsley's clique had claimed them. They all wore glossy pastel leotards. Mine was from the local dance store, long-sleeved, nonshiny, and kelly green. I'd liked it when I picked it out, before I'd learned only losers wore leotards that weren't slick and emblazoned with cool logos. Wearing the same one every day made me even more of a reject. My mom would have bought me another one if I'd asked, but those girls would only have abused me more for trying to fit in. I hated them, but they weren't wrong. I *was* a bug-eyed freak.

"Rotate!" Ms. Carlson called. People started changing equipment stations. My failure to move from the wall was now conspicuous even to me. Reluctantly, I stepped onto the mat and began practicing cartwheels.

My mom had begged me to take this class so that I wouldn't be home by myself all summer. "Are you crazy?" I'd protested. "Girls start taking gymnastics when they're three. They're in the *Olympics* by my age."

"It'll be good exercise and a fun chance to try something new," she'd insisted. "Besides, you know you'll be lonely with me gone all day."

Like I wasn't lonely here.

I turned cartwheels until I was dizzy, my extra-long ponytail alternately dragging on the floor and slapping me in the face. Then I practiced forward rolls along a line on the mat. According to Ms. Carlson, when a person could roll straight along the line, she was ready to roll on the balance beam, but considering that the beam was four inches wide and four feet off the ground, I wasn't planning on trying that. Ever. There was another beam, a practice one, only a few inches off the floor. Maybe, if I was feeling exceptionally lucky, I'd try a roll down that on the last day of class.

After half an eternity, we were dismissed. Pulling shorts on over my leotard, I ran gratefully out of the gym.

I breathed easier outside despite the hot weather. Walking alone down the sidewalk, I felt free in a way I never did at school. Better still, I had five dollars in my pocket. My mom had insisted on working even though I'd begged her to take my birthday off, but she'd felt bad enough about it to come up with ice cream money and lots of promises for later.

I had to cross a parking lot to get to Baskin-Robbins. Heat seeped up through my sneakers and radiated off the parked cars. Not surprisingly, the store's cool interior was packed.

Kendall Karas was at the head of the line. "Lily!" she called, waving me forward.

I hurried up to join her, happy to see a friendly face. "Hi, Kendall. What are you doing here?"

Duh. But Kendall only smiled.

"I'm *thinking* of doing a double," she said. "Bubble gum and . . . yeah. Two scoops of bubble gum. Why mess with perfection?"

The girl behind the counter aimed her dripping scooper at me.

"I'll have a double strawberry," I blurted out. "In a waffle cone, please."

Kendall and I walked outside with our cones, stuffing change into our shorts. "Are you headed home?" I asked hopefully. "We could walk together."

"Okay, but don't tell my mom I was eating ice cream. She'll freak. Especially since we'll be eating it again tonight." Kendall winked. "We *will* be eating it tonight?"

"Definitely. We'll pick you up as soon as my mom gets home from work. Unless . . ." I had an impulsive idea I was almost afraid to say out loud. "Would you want to hang out at my house this afternoon?"

"Can't. I already told Lola I'd be over after lunch." Kendall licked her dripping cone. "Boy drama."

"Right. I mean . . . no biggie," I mumbled, nodding as if that might dislodge the sudden lump in my throat.

You're lucky she's even available tonight, I reminded myself. But my ice cream had become a wobbly pink blur, and I had to blink fast to keep a tear from slipping out.

Kendall Karas was the only friend I'd made in Providence, but Kendall had lots of friends, including a best friend, Lola. They went to the same private school and had known each other forever, which meant that Kendall and I mostly did stuff on our block during the few hours she wasn't busy with Lola. We had tried hanging out as a group once, but Lola didn't like me. I think she probably guessed how badly I wanted to replace her.

"But we'll have fun tonight," Kendall reminded me. "Lucky thirteen! Aren't you excited? My birthday's still two whole months away."

"Yeah. Thirteen. Pretty big." Although so far it hadn't felt that way.

"Are we still having dinner at La Casa Rosa?"

"Why? Would you rather go somewhere else?"

"What? No! I love that place." Kendall transferred a gumball from her cone to her napkin with her front teeth. "It's so hot out today. I wish I hadn't told Lola I'd go over. We could have set up my Slip 'N Slide."

"We still could! Tell her to come over here," I urged. "We can use my yard." Sharing Kendall wasn't nearly as good as having her to myself, but it was way better than being alone.

"She'd never go for it. Too babyish." Kendall sighed. "Lola doesn't get that it's fun sometimes, you know? Just doing stuff like we used to and not talking about her and Jason every second."

"You could tell her."

"That would only hurt her feelings. Besides, you and I'll have fun later. What movie did you choose?"

"I still haven't decided," I lied. I had totally decided, but I'd change my mind in a second if Kendall preferred something else. "There's *Broke and Aimless,* about those slacker treasure hunters. Or *Island Love*—that's supposed to be funny too."

"Yeah." Kendall shrugged. "Either one."

"*Or,*" I said, "we *could* . . . it's only G-rated, but—"

"*Samurai Princess*?" Kendall jumped in. "Would you want to see that, Lily? Because I'm *dying* to and Lola won't go with me. She says animated movies are lame."

She's lame, I thought, keeping my face carefully blank.

"No, wait!" Kendall reversed herself in the next breath. "It's your birthday. You should pick what *you* want to see."

11

"That *is* what I want to see."

"Really? You're not just saying that to make me happy?"

"I'm the one who brought it up."

"True." Kendall swallowed her last bite of ice cream and funneled a rainbow of gumballs into her mouth. "Tonight's going to be so fun. I can't wait!"

But her anticipation was nothing compared to mine. With Kendall I felt like a regular girl, someone actually worth liking. *If only she weren't friends with Lola.*

Our tomb-silent living room released a blast of desert air when I unlocked the front door. I tiptoed nervously through the house, peeking around every corner, then opened a few windows. We'd been renting the place for six months, but the way its floors creaked for no reason still creeped me out. Finally convinced I was alone, I went into the kitchen to microwave a pizza.

The squeaky microwave turntable spun around and around. I checked the clock—12:31. Five hours until my mother got home. I ate my pizza one speck at a time—12:49. Dropping my plate in the sink, I stood and gazed out the kitchen window at the morning glories on our neighbors' fence.

Thirteen years old, I thought. *I wish Gigi were here.* Tears welled up again. My grandmother on my father's side had always promised my thirteenth birthday would be special in ways I couldn't imagine. The last thing I could have imagined was that she wouldn't be here to see it.

The gaping void that was missing Gigi opened wide inside my chest. She'd been gone over a year, and I still couldn't believe she had died, without any warning, without even saying good-bye. My father was killed in an accident before I was two, and Grandma Green had filled in for his side of the family with so much love and attention it was as if she had taken his place. I'd adored her. I still did.

The tears I'd held back all day spilled at last.

Grandma Green had shortened her name to G.G. when I started talking. G.G. eventually became Gigi and stuck. She was the type of grandmother who thought oatmeal cookies were as healthy as the cereal, who let a disaster-prone kid paint pictures in her carpeted living room, and who considered the contents of her walk-in closet one big dress-up wardrobe for her "favorite" (only) grandchild. She collected buttons and pins shaped like clovers in every shade of green, and she wore green most days too. My stays at her house were both frequent and never long enough, always ending with kisses, hugs, and promises of more mischief the next time we got together.

How could a heart so big just give out?

Wiping my tears with both hands, I looked down at my wet palms. A perfect linear scar marked the left one. A week after Gigi's death, my mom and I had gone to her memorial service, then driven home alone for a dinner I couldn't eat. I'd helped wash up, though, and when I dried the knife Mom had used to cut the tomatoes, I accidentally put the sharp edge down instead of up, slicing straight through the dish towel and into my hand. Eight stitches later, Mom was asking the nurse if I needed counseling. She thought I might have cut myself on purpose, but I hadn't; I was just clumsy and sad and not paying attention. I didn't mind the scar, though. It reminded me of Gigi.

Pushing off from the sink, I shuffled down the hall to my bedroom, glad my mom wasn't there to see me crying again. She had never been as fond of Gigi as I was. The knife incident hadn't helped, and when it turned out Gigi hadn't left me any money for college, Mom had turned downright hostile.

"What was the woman thinking?" she'd griped. "She always had plenty of money, so where did it all go? And how does *anyone* her age die without a will?"

It burned my mother up, not getting help with my education when she had such a hard time saving on her salary. But Mom never knew where Gigi's money had come from or even how much she'd really had. Having divorced my father nearly as quickly as she'd married him, she was out of the loop on that stuff.

"I'll tell you this, though," Mom said the day she'd learned no college fund would be coming. "Your grandmother and her son were two of a kind: selfish, impractical dreamers!"

14

Which was why we didn't talk about Gigi anymore—or about my father either.

My bedroom was at the back of the house, out of view from the street and absolutely silent. My pajamas lay the way I'd left them that morning, tossed across my rumpled quilt. The usual assortment of shoes and dirty laundry cluttered the hardwood floor. Passing my desk, I walked into the attached bathroom—the best thing about that house—to take a shower.

Cool water sluiced through my hair and washed away my last tears. Wrapping myself in a towel, I plopped down at my desk and switched on the computer.

No mail—1:03 p.m.

Four and a half more hours until Mom came home and my birthday finally started. I wondered what Kendall would wear to dinner. She always dressed cuter than I did.

I could text her, I thought, reaching for my cell. *But she's probably already with Lola.*

The last thing I needed was Lola saying I couldn't dress myself. I'd just have to figure out my birthday look on my own.

At least I had plenty of time.

I opened my closet. I owned more jeans and tops than dresses, and hardly any dressy shoes. Peering all the way into the back, hunting for the heels I'd worn at Christmas, I spotted my tap shoes. They looked like pumps with ankle straps, and I'd loved wearing them for PE at my old school, even though learning shuffle-ball-change had taken me all semester. Dusting them off, I strapped them onto my bare feet—the way the cool girls had worn theirs. If not for the silver taps on their soles, they could have passed for regular shoes.

Unless I tried to walk somewhere. I took a few loud practice steps on my hardwood floor.

On the last day at my old school, we'd tapped at assembly. I was in the chorus line, which meant I'd lurked in the back and tried not to mess up a few simple steps while the good dancers tapped up a storm. We had all worn the same outfit, though. Dropping the towel, I took that out too: a red-and-white-striped vest top and sequin-spangled blue satin shorts. Those shorts were the sparkliest things I had ever owned, and I kind of loved them. Pulling them on, I added the vest and tapped around my room like a maniac, not caring that I was doing all the steps wrong, just wanting to make some noise in that silent house. I tapped over to my desk and tried to watch myself in the mirror above it, but I couldn't see my feet, only my tangled wet hair and a pale bobbing face turning slowly pink.

I could wear makeup tonight! I thought, stopping dead.

My mom didn't like me to wear more than lip gloss. But I was thirteen now.

And she wasn't home.

Grabbing what makeup I owned from the bathroom, I tapped back over to my desk. My reading light and the big mirror there made a sort of vanity. I lined everything up in a row and started with foundation, but the base made my pale skin look pasty against my nearly black hair. I counteracted that by piling on pink blush. Breaking out the liquid eyeliner, I tried painting thin lines against my lashes. That brush was tricky, though, and before I got both sides even, I looked like Cleopatra. With a sunburn. I was headed to the bathroom to wash my face when the doorbell rang.

Kendall! I thought, whirling around. My tap shoes clattered crazily as I ran through the house. I threw the front door open, but nobody was there, only the Douglases' Great Dane doing doughnuts through Ms. Clark's sprinkler. That was when I noticed the package lying beneath our mailbox, a brown-paper-wrapped package addressed to Lilybet Green.

I had no clue who that box was from. Looking back, I definitely could have devoted more thought to waiting for Mom to get home. But it was my birthday. And I started ripping.

Ka-boom!

Sparkling . . . Twinkling . . .

Black.

Chapter 2

I woke up flat on my back on our front porch, surrounded by worried neighbors. For a moment I blinked up into their freaked-out faces and wondered what they were doing there.

Then I remembered.

"Ohhh," I groaned. "My head!"

I reached to touch the spot that had thunked against the boards, but Mrs. Douglas grabbed my wrist, stopping my hand.

"Lily!" she cried. "Thank God! Don't move." Her twin toddler boys peered at me from around her back. "I've called nine-one-one, and your mother. Lie still until they get here."

"My mother?" I repeated, confused. An odor like gunpowder mixed with scorched feathers filled my nose, and my voice sounded oddly dull, as if I were hearing myself through a wall. "She's at work."

"Don't try to think, hon—you probably have a concussion. Harley!" Her crazy Great Dane had loped into our yard, barking his head off. "Harley, shut up! I swear to Pete!"

"How many fingers am I holding up?" Mr. Lopez asked, waving gnarled knuckles before my eyes at a speed that made my head ache.

"Um, maybe if you could hold them still . . ."

"The paramedics will do that, Al," Mrs. Karas said. She had the same china blue eyes as Kendall, although those were hard to focus on too. "What in the world happened, Lily? It sounded like something exploded."

I turned my head side to side on the boards. Our living room window was a spiderweb of cracks; a chunk of glass near its center was missing. The only traces of the mysterious package were some shredded scraps of brown paper.

"It was just a little . . . a . . . um," I fumbled. I had forgotten the word for *box*.

"Here, Lily, you dropped this." Mrs. Douglas pressed something warm into my hand, letting go of my wrist so I could raise it to my face. I blinked, then closed my eyes and squeezed them hard. The item I was holding was . . . not possible.

But when I dared to open my eyes again, there it was, clutched so hard my knuckles were white.

Gigi's key! I thought, stunned.

All my life, my grandmother had worn the same necklace, an ornate gold key on an intricately woven chain. The key looked old-fashioned, like something that might have opened a long-ago mansion, but three sparkling emeralds along its shaft suggested it had never been used in a door. I'd been fascinated by it since I was a baby, latching on with a chubby fist anytime Gigi bent near.

"Like that, do you?" she'd always said with a twinkle in her wide-set eyes. "Well, of course you do! And someday it will be yours, Lilybet. You'll wear the key, I promise." But after Gigi died, we couldn't find her necklace. The key had just disappeared.

Until now.

Part of my staggered brain understood that the necklace must have been inside the exploding box. But how? And why? It didn't make any sense.

"Whoa, dude! What *was* that?" a new voice asked. I glanced up to see Byron Berry join the circle of faces above me. "Cherry bomb? M-eighty? *Dude,* it was awesome! Where did you get it?"

Byron was the cutest boy in our neighborhood and, as far as I knew, all of the adjoining ones. He was older than me, tougher than me, and orders of magnitude cooler. I'd had a hopeless crush on him from the day I'd moved in.

This was not the first impression I'd dreamed of making.

"I have to go," I blurted out, struggling to sit up.

The porch whirled dizzily.

"You need to lie still for the ambulance," Mrs. Douglas said, trying gently to press me back down. "We don't know if you're hurt yet."

"I'm fine." I wasn't at all sure about that, but the ringing in my ears was clearing, and sitting upright had swept away some of the gunpowder smell. "I really have to go."

"I don't think it's a good idea—" Mrs. Karas began, but Mr. Lopez cut her off.

"Ladies, she has to use the facilities. When you've got to go, you've got to go. Right, Lily?"

Byron grinned. I felt my face heat up. But even having Byron Berry think I had bladder issues was preferable to having him see me laid out like this.

"That's right, Mr. Lopez." Somehow I got to my feet, my taps clattering on the boards. That was when I remembered what I was wearing. And my damp, unbrushed hair. And the makeup. *Oh, please, no, the makeup!*

"Lily!" Mrs. Douglas's footsteps lagged behind mine

21

as I turned and dashed through our open front door and down the hall to my bedroom, locking the door behind me.

"Lily!" she called again, jiggling the knob. "You should *not* be running! The ambulance is coming."

"I'll be out in a second. I just have to . . ." What? Think? Wash my face? Die of embarrassment? Kicking off my tap shoes, I ran into the bathroom.

The sight that greeted me in the mirror took my breath away. The source of that scorched feathers smell was now appallingly clear. Long clumps of once-glossy hair stuck out forlornly between patches singed back to my scalp. Black residue from the blast clung to the edges of my face, making the center part extra pale. And then there was the eyeliner.

I looked like a goth struck by lightning.

Tears flowed down my cheeks, leaving black tracks. I have freakishly wide-set eyes and a pointy chin. I'm far too odd-looking to be vain, but my hair was my one good feature, shiny and thick all the way down my back. Now half of it was stubble and the rest would have to be cut. Choking back a sob, I reached for a washcloth and realized Gigi's key was still clutched in my hand.

I stopped crying instantly, examining the key in the bathroom light and trying to make sense of its sudden appearance. I had no idea where it had come from, but Gigi had always meant for me to have it, and now, somehow, I did. With shaking hands, I slipped its chain over my head.

The key hung low on my chest, where my cleavage would have been if I'd had any. Staring into the mirror, I vowed to never take it off. Then I grabbed the soap and scrubbed my face. Surprisingly, considering the state of my hair, my skin wasn't damaged at all. But I didn't have time to ponder that. If someone forced me to go to the hospital, I didn't intend to make the trip in sequined tap-dancing shorts. Hurrying into my bedroom, I dashed toward my closet and froze.

There was a little man standing on my bed.

Eighteen inches tall at most, he wore a black pilgrim hat, a green coat with silver buttons, tight black britches, and black boots with buckles, all of which looked as if they had just come through a freak rainstorm. Hanging down over his crossed arms was a wiry beard, a wild mess of blond whiskers with the merest hint of green, as if he'd been swimming in chlorine all summer. His eyes were green as well. They pinned mine so intently I couldn't look away.

"Oh no," I moaned. "I *do* have a concussion."

The little man huffed with amusement, his arms rising on his round belly. "I've been called a few things in my day, but never a concussion."

I shook my head and blinked. He was still there, his boots stomping dents in my quilt as he walked closer. I smelled pipe smoke and grass and . . . wet dog?

"Hello, Lilybet," he said.

"You kn-kn-know my name?"

"O' course! Now, don't go all shaky, Lil. And don't you dare scream or you'll tetch us up good."

My desk chair rolled across the floor and hit me behind the knees. Looking down, I saw two more rain-spattered little men pushing it, virtual clones of the first one except for the lack of beards on their pointed chins. I collapsed onto the seat, pretty sure I was hallucinating.

"You're not real," I said. "I mean, seriously. I'm imagining you guys, right?"

"We're as real as that key you're wearing, girl. Where do you think it came from?"

"I . . . I . . . This can't be healthy."

The bearded one jumped to the floor, bowing till his whiskers brushed wood. "Lilybet Green, we come to welcome you home on behalf o' the Clan o' Green. I am your humble brother Balthazar Green."

The other two lined up beside him and bowed as well. "Welcome, Lilybet. Your brother Maxwell Green," the second one said.

"Your brother Caspar Green," offered the third.

I gripped the arms of my chair hard. Their corners dug into my palms, suggesting that I was still conscious.

"Um . . . no offense, guys," I got out, "but I'm an only child."

"Depends how you look at it," Balthazar said. "Now pack up and let's be off. We've already drawn more attention than we want." He turned a withering gaze on Maxwell.

Maxwell hung his head. "That package wasn't supposed to explode."

"Yes it was," Caspar muttered.

"Well, to be sure." Maxwell gave me a pleading look. "But it wasn't supposed to *hurt* you, Lil. Cain said it would just add a bit o' flash."

"Flash?" I repeated uncertainly.

"Flair," Caspar supplied. "Excitement. Proper ceremony."

"But your hair . . ." Maxwell wrung his hands. "That is a shame."

"Well, it can't be helped now." Balthazar shook his head. "Although frankly, Lil, I'm surprised. Who could have guessed you'd turn out to be so delicate?"

"Deli-*what*?" I sputtered. "I just survived a *bomb*!"

"That bitty pop o' sparks? All right, all right! Let's not split hairs," he responded at my outraged expression. "Not any *more* hairs, I mean. I'm afraid we're off on the wrong foot, Lil. You do realize your grandmother sent us?"

"My grandmother?" I said with disbelief.

He pointed to the key around my neck. "Maureen was one o' our own—but, then, you called her Gigi, right? We've been holding that key for your thirteenth birthday, just like we promised we would."

"Gigi gave *you* her key?"

"In a manner o' speaking. It's a long story, Lil, and she'd definitely want you to hear it. So put on some shoes and let's go."

"But—"

"I know someone who can fix that hair for you," Maxwell wheedled. "A bit o' magic will grow it back good as new."

"Really?" I asked hopefully.

"We'll just nip home, then nip right back," Balthazar promised. "Won't take a minute."

"Well . . . if you're positive I'll be home before my mother gets—"

The wail of a siren cut through my words, snapping me back to my senses. What was I agreeing to? My mom would be home any second, and these little green men could only be figments of my explosion-scrambled brain.

The siren swelled louder. I heard Mrs. Douglas calling out front. Considering that I was conversing with my imagination, maybe medical attention wasn't such a bad idea after all.

"You guys have to leave now," I said, standing up to move toward my closet. "I have to change into some normal clothes, and if anyone catches me talking to you, I'll wind up in a rubber room."

"By all that glitters, girl! Don't be difficult!" Balthazar exclaimed. "We're not leaving without you. Why else are we here?"

"Don't ask me. I'm not even sure you *are* here."

We faced off in a four-way stare-down. And then I noticed something that made the peach fuzz prickle down my spine. Slowly, barely perceptibly, all three were creeping closer.

"I *can't*," I pleaded uneasily. "What would I tell my mom?"

"Don't tell her anything," Caspar suggested. "Let her think you ran away. That usually works grand."

"Usually? You guys have done this before?"

Balthazar whipped a glare in Caspar's direction.

"Um . . . no," Caspar stammered. "Not this. Exactly."

They eased another inch closer.

"Moooooom!" I shouted. "Mrs. Douglas! Help!"

All three of them jumped me at once. Six legs ran circles around mine. Hands reached above my knees, tying me up with a gold chain barely thicker than fishing line. Trying to kick free, I lost my balance and crashed to the floor. They buzzed about like frenzied green bees, able to reach all of me now.

"Knock it off!" I shouted, slapping and struggling. "Stop!"

"Not to worry, Lil. We'll be out o' here in a jiffy," Balthazar huffed.

It was far from a fair fight, especially with me still half dazed by that blast on the porch. In seconds, they had tied my wrists together and bound my arms to my body, trussing me up like a sausage.

"If there's anything you'll be needing in the next few days," Balthazar said, "you'd best name it now."

"*Days!* You said we'd be gone a *minute!*" I tried to sit up, but they had me so hog-tied I could barely wiggle. I'd have to talk my way out of it.

"Look, this is obviously a big misunderstanding," I said, forcing down my rising panic. "If Gigi sent you guys, of course I'll go. Just untie me so I can put on some shoes and we'll go wherever you want."

Balthazar held my gaze for a long moment. Then he threw back his head and laughed. "Bit o' a liar, are you, Lil? You're a Green, all right! Get the door, Caspar."

Removing a coiled rope from his jacket, Caspar lassoed my doorknob and flicked the door open. No one was in the hall. In a flash, the three of them wriggled beneath me and hoisted me over their heads like a surfboard. Something about the way they'd tied me up would not let me bend at all.

"Mrs. Douglas!" I bellowed again. *"Help!"*

"On my mark, lads," Balthazar said. "Ready . . . go!" They marched in unison, carrying me faceup.

"Seriously! Stop it!" I begged. "This isn't funny anymore. Besides, do you really think you can carry me past all those people outside?"

"What a leprechaun carries is invisible, Lil. Everyone knows that," Caspar said.

"'What a . . .' Did you say *leprechaun*?"

My bedroom doorframe brushed my head and popped me in the shoulder. "Oopsie!" Balthazar trilled. "Mind the corners, laddies."

They hustled me down the hall, through the kitchen, and into the den, where Caspar withdrew from my midsection long enough to repeat his lasso trick on the back doorknob. Footsteps entered the living room. Voices called my name.

"Help!" I hollered as three leprechauns ran me headfirst through the open back door into the sunshine outside.

"Watch the stairs!" Balthazar barked. "Lively now, lads!"

We jolted down the three back steps, around the corner of the house, and through our side yard toward the street. An ambulance was parked at the curb, its emergency lights revolving. Mrs. Douglas and the other neighbors stood on our porch, waving an EMT across the lawn. My body cleared the driveway just as my mother's Civic pulled in. She was out before the car stopped rolling, leaving her driver's door open.

"Lily!" she cried, sprinting right past me on her way to the porch. "Lily!"

"Mom!" I shouted desperately. "Mom, help!"

She rushed into the house without even turning her head. None of the neighbors glanced my way either as the leprechauns ran me over our grass to the sidewalk.

"Help!" I screamed. "Why doesn't anyone answer me?"

"That'll be the binding gold, Lil," Balthazar's voice said beneath me. "A bit o' magic there—immobility, plus it makes you completely silent to anyone outside the clan. Hated to use it, but you forced us a bit. The end will justify the means—you'll see. Bear to the left, lads, into the street!"

They trotted me down the bike lane in broad daylight, past houses and cars and pedestrians. Nobody noticed us. Nobody heard a thing. My mind raced with the need to get free, but my body was paralyzed. Panicky tears jiggled down my upturned face as block after block slipped by.

"Bal . . . Bal . . . Balty," Maxwell wheezed. "I've got . . . to put . . . her down."

"Not yet!" Balthazar huffed, out of breath himself. "Almost . . . there."

We bumped up over the curb and into my neighborhood park, running practically under the noses of the Mommy-and-me crew at the sandbox. Sunshine blazed into my face, searing past wet lashes.

"To the rocket! The rocket ship!" Balthazar cried.

By then it wouldn't have shocked me if they were space

aliens too, but when they jogged around the back of the park's maintenance hut, I saw what they were talking about.

A huge play rocket ship lay on its side, its disassembled metal legs rusting in a heap. The leprechauns charged in through the rocket's open base, carrying me headfirst. For a split second, I welcomed the shade. Then the stifling heat trapped inside hit me like a frying pan.

"This'll do," Balthazar panted. "Heave ho, laddies."

Three pairs of hands thrust upward at once. For a moment, I was airborne. Then I hit the curved floor of the fake rocket like a sack of bowling balls.

"Ow!" I cried. "Why are you doing this?"

"Sorry, Lil," Balthazar said. "Can't be helped."

"I'm pretty sure it can! Take me home!"

"We're working on it," he assured me. "Just as fast as we know how."

"I can't breathe. It's a million degrees in here!"

"At least," Maxwell agreed, wiping his dripping face on his green coat sleeve.

Balthazar's face was flushed purple above his full beard. "We'll just be here a moment. Give us a chance to regroup."

"I'm for opening a door," Caspar said.

"And how do you propose doing that before the trial?" Balthazar asked. "Use your bean, lad, I'm begging."

"We'll have to whistle for the cart," Maxwell said.

"Whistle away!" Caspar invited sarcastically. "It's only three miles off. We should have told Fizz to wait here."

"Right," Maxwell retorted. "Because none of these humans would have noticed six dogs and a—"

"By every coin and nugget!" Balthazar shouted. "If the pair o' you don't shut up and start helping me, I'll have you both before the council!"

They all fell momentarily silent, glaring at each other.

"It's so hot in here," I moaned. My head throbbed from its second fall to the floor, and the air felt like lava in my lungs. "Can't you just take me home?"

The leprechauns glanced at me, then resumed their argument, debating furiously about doors and dogs and doughnuts. Nothing they said made sense anymore. And although I was still afraid, my eyes wouldn't stay open. Maybe it was more magic from their binding gold, or maybe it was the normal result of being concussed and abducted, but I felt myself drifting and then I was gone, sucked into the bottomless depths of a velvety green darkness.

32

Chapter 3

I was awakened by a jolt that shuddered through my bones.

"Hie!" a voice cried out. "Pull!"

I struggled to open my eyes, but my lids were still so heavy I could barely manage a slit. The sunshine had been snuffed out, replaced by a dim green glow.

Muffled voices floated back to me on a whiff of pipe smoke.

". . . desperate glad to have her with us at last, but I hope she bucks up soon, because there never was a set o' tests like this. To pit her against the Scarlets . . ."

"Aye, but Wee Kylie! What match is a lad for a lass? If she's an ounce o' Maureen in her, she'll prevail. The council knows how to run a trial."

"Would I be disloyal enough to suggest they don't? But this one's not off to a grand start. . . ."

Balthazar and Maxwell were deep in yet another conversation that made no sense. The air surrounding us now was cool and damp. Water dripped nearby, a slow pinging plop. I forced my eyes open at last.

I was lying propped on my back in a pile of fresh-cut grass mounded on a flat wagon. The wagon was a little bigger than a cot, with a low wooden railing around three sides and wheels like four extra-wide bicycle tires. At the forward ends of the railing, green lanterns hung from pegs, casting their strange glow over a team of six shaggy dogs the size of Labrador retrievers. They were pulling me through a long, dark cave, its low ceiling dripping from dirty crags to a muddy floor below.

"Hie!" the voice I had wakened to called again, urging the dogs on through the mud.

The team's paws made sucking sounds as they struggled to pull the cart forward. Their hind ends scrabbled and bunched, stretching their harnesses tight. The wagon jolted again, lurching forward as the muck released it and we rolled out onto hard stone. I bounced awkwardly in the grass. Then, slowly, I sat up.

Balthazar and Maxwell were riding bareback on the pair of dogs nearest me. Caspar and a fourth leprechaun were riding the lead pair. Judging by my surroundings, I'd been asleep for a long time.

"Where are you taking me?" I asked. My voice echoed loudly, shaky and scared.

Balthazar turned on his shaggy mount, straddling it backward to face me. "Look who's awake!" he said cheerfully, knocking spent tobacco out of his pipe. "Fizz! Here's your chance to say hello."

The new leprechaun sprang to his feet on his trotting dog's back, riding like a circus performer. "Lilybet Green! At last!" he said, bowing down to his boots. "I am your humble brother and dog skipper, Fizz."

He was so obviously pleased to meet me that it seemed wrong to be rude. "Um . . . hi," I returned.

Fizz straightened up, beaming. Then, with an easy leap, he spun in the air and landed restraddling his mount, catching its ears like reins.

Fizz could totally roll on the balance beam, I thought, temporarily distracted.

Balthazar leaned toward me over his dog's tail. "First ride in a dog cart, Lil?"

"That isn't obvious?" I retorted, feeling no obligation to be polite to Balthazar. I rubbed my wrists where he'd tied them, only then realizing that the binding gold was gone.

35

My heart revved faster. There was nothing to keep me from running away!

Nothing except total darkness. Beyond the glow of the cart's green lanterns, the cave we were rolling through was pitch-black and seemingly endless. The thought of running through it blind was truly terrifying.

Maybe I can snag one of those lanterns. If I jumped off and grabbed the light fast, I could run back the way we'd just come. Although, I wasn't a bit convinced I could outrun the leprechauns. They were small, but they'd already proven they were ridiculously strong for their size. And what if they sent the dogs after me? For all I knew, we were miles underground, and I got winded halfway around the school track.

"Where are we going?" I asked.

"Home, Lil! To the Meadows. Your grandmother, Maureen, was our keeper, and now you'll take her place—as soon as you pass your trial, o' course. But that's only one wee bitty test, and then we'll all live happily ever after."

"You're taking me to *live* with you?"

"Don't say it like that, Lil," Balthazar replied, offended. "It's an honor, isn't it? One we've been well put out reserving for you—even before this nightmare o' a trip to fetch you. You might show a bit o' gratitude."

"Gratitude? For *kidnapping* me?"

Maxwell had been following the conversation over his

shoulder. Now he turned backward on his dog too. "Maybe we should explain from the beginning."

"You could try," I said sulkily.

"All right, then." Balthazar pulled out his pipe and lit it again. The dogs settled into a rhythm, loping along the cave floor with the cart rolling smoothly behind them. "Here it is," Balthazar said, exhaling a perfect smoke ring. "You, my girl, have leprechaun blood, on your father's side."

"What?" My jaw worked up and down. "What are you trying to say? That I'm some sort of *leprechaun*?"

Balthazar grinned around his pipe stem. "Do you *look* like a leprechaun, Lil? Your eyes and chin are right enough, but have you seen the rest o' you? Ninety-nine percent human, you are, give or take."

"You're a lepling," Maxwell offered. "One o' our sisters on the human side."

"Gee, thanks. That makes everything clear."

"Aye, but you're far luckier than most," Balthazar said. "Most leplings go their whole lives not realizing they're a bit more than meets the eye. A fine rare privilege it is, being called to join the clan."

I didn't feel privileged. I felt scared and confused and more than a little angry.

"Your grandmother," he went on, "had the honor o' being our keeper. That gold you're wearing is the Greens' keeper key. Maureen always intended to hand it on to you, but a keeper has to be o' age—thirteen at the youngest—and our poor Maureen passed on before you were old enough. It's been a hard road this past year, carrying on without a keeper, but we waited for you, Lil, because to try for the key and the cottage is your birthright."

"Cottage? Wait, are you telling me Gigi lived with you?" Now I knew they were lying. Hadn't I been to her house about a million times?

"Aye, that she did, when she wanted to," Balthazar said. "She came and went, as keepers do."

I was about to call Balthazar a liar to his face when I remembered something. I'd spent a lot of time with Gigi, but Mom had often complained about how hard Gigi was to reach when we were trying to set up a visit. "I call the woman, I e-mail, but she's off who-knows-where again, pulling another of her disappearing acts. Really, Lily, sometimes it makes me wonder if it's safe leaving you with her. You might *both* disappear someday."

Even so, I found it hard to believe that Gigi was off in some meadow, keeping leprechauns.

"So now you've come at last," Balthazar said, "although I do think Maureen might have warned us how stubborn you are. It was dangerous enough showing up to collect you without all that fuss you raised. You may not appreciate, Lilybet, how easily we could have been captured."

"Captured!" I exclaimed, hooting so loudly I spooked the dogs. "Who would want to capture *you*?"

"Don't be ignorant, girl. Everyone wants to catch a leprechaun."

"Right," I said. "For your Lucky Charms."

Balthazar's eyes narrowed, not a hint of humor about them. "For our gold."

"How do people even see you? I thought you were invisible."

"O' course we're not invisible! You see us, don't you? But most full-blooded humans don't take us in somehow—us *or* what we carry."

"Psychics see us," Maxwell offered. "And drunks, although no one ever believes them. Most of them don't believe it themselves, once they sober up."

"I can sympathize."

"Lucky for us," Balthazar said, "true psychics are rare, and your average drunk can't catch his own elbow. Still, there's always the danger o' crossing paths with another lepling. They're more common than you might think, especially in California. Not that a body has to see us to trample us. And let's not forget their dogs! Why do humans always raise such snarling, ill-mannered mutts? Do you know that a great vicious beast chased us off your front porch right through your neighbor's lawn fountain? Make no mistake, Lil, all manner o' dangerous creatures see us plain as pumpkins."

"You should have stayed home, then, safe and sound," I said. "That would have been A-OK with me."

Balthazar took a deep breath and let it out slowly, determined not to be baited. "Ach, Lil. When we get to the Meadows, you'll change your tune. The whole clan is waiting to welcome you home. You are going to be one very important girl."

"Yeah? What's a keeper do anyway? Am I some sort of leprechaun queen?"

"Our queen!" Balthazar's braying laughter echoed through the cave. "Oh me, that's rich. Caspar! Fizz! Lil thinks she's our queen!"

I glared at him in a fury. I was missing my thirteenth birthday because of him, and now he was making fun of me too. No dinner, no movie, no ice cream, no Kendall . . .

"I want to go home," I said, a sudden quaver in my voice. "You guys are mean, and you made me miss my party."

Balthazar stopped braying and put on a conciliatory tone. "Now, Lil, don't be upset. Someday we'll laugh about this, you and I. And as far as parties go, aren't we throwing you one this very night?"

"You're throwing me a party," I said, not believing a single word. "And who's going to be there?"

"Why, everyone, o' course! The entire Clan o' Green. Do you like cheese and doughnuts, Lil? O' course you do—you're a Green, aren't you?" he went on before I could answer. "And we couldn't have a party without piping. The acoustics in Green Field are the envy o' the clans! You'll see, Lilybet. You'll see it all."

"You said if I went with you, we'd come right back, and we've already been gone for hours," I accused, not exactly sure how long I'd been unconscious. "You lied. You all did."

"Aye, perhaps a wee bit," he admitted with an unrepentant grin. "But trust me on this, Lil: your grandmother wanted you with us today more than anything in the world."

I stared him down, on the verge of tears. The leprechauns obviously had no intention of taking me home, and how could I trust what they said about Gigi when they'd lied about everything else? Sinking back on the grass, I closed my eyes and tried to think.

I would have to get home on my own. But how?

I didn't have a clue.

Silent tears seeped out and dripped off my cheeks. I hated myself for being so weak and scared and useless. Ainsley Williams had never been abducted and held by leprechauns—I felt certain of that.

The dog cart rumbled on. With every turn of its wheels, I was getting farther from home, but instead of inspiring me to some brilliant plan, the stress turned my brain to mush. Hours passed. My mom was going to be worried sick, my explanation of where I'd been would probably get me grounded for life, and I still couldn't think of a single way to help myself.

"Almost there now," Balthazar sang out, abruptly breaking the silence. "You won't want to miss this, Lil."

My body swayed as the cart made a hard right turn.

"Hie! Hie! Home!" Fizz called excitedly.

The dogs broke into a run, creating a breeze that blew out both lanterns. We charged onward through darkness so dense I couldn't see my own hands. I screamed, certain we were about to crash.

But Balthazar only chuckled. "Not to worry, Lil!" he reassured me. "The dogs know where they're going."

I was too freaked out to do anything but hang on.

Very gradually, light began to bleed into the blackness. I made out silhouettes—first my fingers, then Balthazar's and Maxwell's tall hats. They were facing forward now and holding on. The entire team slowly became visible, with Caspar and Fizz still up front, skippering the charging dogs.

"Hie! Hie!" Fizz yelled.

The dogs put on even more speed. The cart careened crazily as the trickle of distant light grew into an eerie green glow. We were traveling through a huge natural tunnel, its walls slanting together to join in a peaked ceiling high above my head. The tunnel floor began to slope uphill, forming a rocky horizon against the growing light. Fizz and

Caspar sat their mounts like cowboys galloping into a green sunset.

"That's the way, lads!" Balthazar cried happily. Maxwell clutched two fistfuls of fur as if his life depended on it.

At the crest of the rise, the tunnel's walls bent sharply away from us. I made out an enormous new cavern, its ceiling dripping with pale green stalactites as far as the eye could see. Then the cart tilted downward again, and I got my first glimpse of the cavern floor.

Hundreds of leprechauns crowded a chamber so vast its edges were lost to darkness. A sea of black hats teemed beneath us, lit by hundreds of greenish torches held aloft in tiny hands.

Putting two fingers to his mouth, Balthazar unleashed a piercing whistle. "Oy, oy, oy!" he shouted.

A roar rose up to greet us as the crowd below caught sight of our wagon. They surged in our direction, boots thundering on the stony floor, torches bobbing wildly.

"What did I tell you?" Balthazar crowed, glancing back at me. "There's no place like home, Lil!"

A deafening explosion rocked the cave. Brilliant green sparks flew through the air, twinkling against the crystalline ceiling and showering the cheering crowd below.

"There's so many of them!" I gasped. "What are they all doing here?"

"Came to welcome you home, didn't they?"

The dog cart moved down through the frenzied crowd, its team completely unruffled by the fireworks exploding overhead or the mob of leprechauns crowding the wagon.

"Lilybet!" they shouted, doffing their pilgrim hats and waving them alongside their torches. "Lilybet Green! Welcome!"

I shrank into my mound of wilted grass. The cart had slowed to a crawl. I could finally see well enough to make a run for it. . . .

But where was I supposed to go?

Trapped and seriously outnumbered, I decided it might be safest to play along, at least until I came up with a plan. Taking a deep breath, I lifted one hand in a hesitant wave.

My weak gesture was greeted by a roar. A shout went up to the stalactites: "Green! Green! *Greeeeeeeeen!*"

"What did I tell you, Lil?" Balthazar boasted, sitting taller on his prancing mutt.

The crowd pressed in from all sides, forcing the cart to a crawl. Torchlight flickered on hundreds of upturned faces, many of them bearded and all with lively, wide-set green eyes. And not all the faces belonged to men. There were women in the crowd, too, although few and far between. They wore ankle-high boots with intricate silver buckles, fitted green coats that flared at the hips, and low, broad-brimmed hats rolled up on one side, secured with silver pins and sweeping green feathers.

Fizz and Caspar stood on their dogs' backs, waving for the crowd to give the cart room. Balthazar just waved, clearly loving the attention.

Maxwell finally relaxed his hold on his dog's fur and smiled over his shoulder at me. "Only a little farther," he promised.

On the other side of the cavern, our cart led the parade into a slit of a low-ceilinged tunnel. Water dripped from the ceiling, plopping on my head and making the torches behind us sizzle. The walls closed in until they scraped the cart. The roof descended by degrees.

"Might want to lie down for this next bit, Lil," Balthazar said. "That is, if you don't want to bump your bean."

Lying flat in the wilted grass, I watched dark, slimy rock pass inches above my face. I had never been claustrophobic before, but suddenly I could barely breathe. A horrible whimpering reached my ears before I realized I was making it. I was one second from a total meltdown when the ceiling finally rose back up.

But the walls squeezed in even closer.

"Here's where things get tight," Fizz said, sliding off his mount. "We're going to need you out of the wagon, Lil, so we can tilt her up and through."

Caspar, Balthazar, and Maxwell helped unhitch the team. Reluctantly, I lowered my bare feet to the ground and stood up.

The stone felt cold and slick on my soles as I ventured a few paces forward. The torches were so far behind me now that the passage was almost pitch-dark. Glancing back, I saw the upended cart plugging the tunnel like a cork in a bottle, everyone but my abductors still stuck behind it. Fizz tended to the dogs while Balthazar, Caspar, and Maxwell worked with the leprechauns behind them to tilt the wagon through on its side.

No one was paying attention to me. This was my chance.

My feet slid quickly through the mucky darkness, my heart skipping with fear. They'd have that cart through in a few minutes, and then they'd be looking for me. I moved as fast as I dared, slipping blindly, cringing at each drop of water that fell on my head. I groped desperately for a place to hide, for any sort of escape. . . .

A hint of light seeped toward me from the tunnel's far end. I hesitated, thinking I must be approaching another torch-filled cavern. Then I caught a whiff of pine and almost lost my mind.

That was *sunlight*! I was headed *outside*!

"Yes!" I yelped, breaking into a sprint. My feet slid and slithered on the cave floor as I flung myself toward the light, only one thought on my mind: escape.

"Lil!" Balthazar shouted. "Lil, you wait for us!"

I could already taste fresh air, full of sunshine and pollen and grass. I dashed on like a maniac.

"Lil!" Balthazar hollered.

Birds sang up ahead. In one final, breakneck sprint, I burst out through the cave's jagged exit. . . .

And stood blinking in a fairy-tale forest.

Beams of light slanted through the trees and sparkled on a blanket of dewy green clover, each leaf facing into the rising sun. Tiny white flowers rose on slender stalks, dripping diamonds of dew. Not a footstep disturbed that silver blanket. No planes flew overhead. There wasn't the least sign of a building, or sidewalk, or road.

"Uh-oh," I said, completely lost. "I don't think we're in Providence anymore."

Chapter 4

66"What did I tell you?" Balthazar boasted. "The Meadows is the grandest place in all creation! Wave to the folk, Lil. Smile!"

I was riding in the dog cart again, being pulled down the center of the strangest, most beautiful valley I could have imagined. Pink wisps of clouds drifted across the yellow sun in a perfect aqua sky. A mile to either side of the wagon, dense trees covered steep hillsides. And down the rolling center of the valley was one long meadow of green grass and billowing clover punctuated by a few giant oaks. Their spreading branches shaded colonies of leprechaun-sized, slightly crooked three-story dwellings with green lace curtains and eager hands waving from every window. Once I'd emerged from the cave and realized I had nowhere to run, I'd reluctantly climbed back into the cart, letting Balthazar and the huge crowd trailing on foot believe I'd been so thrilled to see the Meadows that I'd dashed ahead out of excitement. I hadn't given up, though. As soon as I saw a landmark belonging to the real world, I intended to bolt again.

"How long have I been gone now?" I asked, glancing pointlessly at my wrist. I did own a watch, but of course I hadn't been smart enough to ask for it—or my phone—when the leprechauns snatched me. I could only guess I'd been missing for twenty-four hours, maybe even longer. "My mom'll be psychoballistic."

"No point worrying about what can't be helped," Balthazar told me jovially. "Plenty o' time to deal with that later."

"Easy for you to say. You're not the one who'll be grounded until you turn forty."

He laughed annoyingly. "I'll wager that when you get home, you'll find your mum less worried than you thought she'd be. So wave to the folk, girl! Show some manners!"

I shut my mouth and waved, hating him silently.

A long, bumpy ride later, the landscape began to change. The houses clustered closer together, gradually forming a sprawling storybook village. The dirt road sprouted cobblestones. I waved to the mostly male leprechauns pouring into the streets and was greeted by a roar of *"Greeeeeeeeen!"*

"That's the way!" Balthazar said, waving wildly himself.

Ahead of us in the village, green streamers festooned the streets and swung in the breeze between crooked town-homes. Our cart moved forward through throngs of leprechauns waving hats, handkerchiefs, and handfuls of clover arranged like bouquets. At the center of town, where the buildings crowded close enough to bump into each other, the dogs took a sharp left down a new lane, one with a human-sized house at its end.

The thatched one-story cottage dwarfed the leprechaun houses, its little square of front lawn starting at the last row of cobblestones. I scrambled out of the wagon as the lower half of the cottage's green front door opened and three female leprechauns filed out.

The woman in front was obviously the oldest, with streaks of white in her greenish blond hair. The buckles on her shoes were shaped like oversized silver bows, and the curved feathers pinned to her hat were nearly as long as she was. The woman behind her had a flounce on her coat and a bouncy step to match. And the last of the group was a teenager with waist-length hair and a shy, eager glint in her wide green eyes.

"Welcome, Lilybet!" the oldest one called. "It took you

long enough," she scolded in an aside to Balthazar. "Where have you been? Touring the whole countryside soaking up your five minutes of glory?"

"Well, now, Bronny," he replied uncomfortably. "We had a few unexpected hiccups."

"You know the banquet is tonight! Yet here you are, as late as dawn after a nightmare, barely giving us time to get ready at all!"

"Can we talk about this later?" he begged.

"Aye. That we will," she promised before bowing her head to me. "Your sister Bronwyn," she said. "Welcome, Lilybet."

The other two women dropped curtsies behind her.

"Kate," said the second in line.

"Your sister Lexie," the youngest one ventured. "'Tis an honor, Lilybet."

"Well, come in, girl. Come in!" Bronwyn said, herding me toward the door. "Your banquet starts in a few hours, and we've got fixing up to do before then." She shook her head disapprovingly. "More fixing than I'd expected."

"I don't usually dress this way," I said, cringing under her scrutiny. "And what happened to my hair was *not* my fault."

"No, I daresay it wasn't," she agreed. "Menfolk! Well, come along, Lilybet. The four of us will set things right."

The cottage's front door was farmhouse-style, with upper and lower halves. The leprechaun women walked inside through the open bottom section. Without a single glance back at Balthazar, I opened the door's top half and followed them in.

Half-burned green candles sat on ledges around every wall. A lumpy-looking bed lay beneath a comforter next to a tall cupboard. The room's center held a square table surrounded by three tall stools with ladder-rung legs and a normal, human-sized chair. But the most surprising feature was a claw-foot iron bathtub half hidden behind a wooden screen. Curling steam rose from its water, scenting the air with cloves.

"Dive in," Bronwyn offered, following my gaze. "We're going to have tea, but that can wait." She wrinkled her small nose. "We'll probably enjoy it more after you've had a wash anyway."

That seemed like a low blow, but she wasn't wrong. My blue satin shorts were a mess—dirty, wrinkled, and as covered with grass stains as my bare legs. My striped vest was in even worse shape. And then there was my hair, which had to be the sorriest sight of all. I took a step toward the tub and stopped. "I don't have anything clean to put on."

"Right here, Lil." Lexie ran to the cupboard and pulled on a tassel attached to its door. The door swung open to reveal human-sized clothes on hangers, some of which I recognized.

"That's Gigi's sweater!" I cried, crossing the room in

three bounds. "And those sneakers! I remember those! Why do you have her things?"

"Balthazar didn't explain?" Bronwyn sounded annoyed again. "This is the keeper's hut, Lil. Maureen left them here."

Grabbing a pole with a hook on its end, Lexie snagged the hanger holding a green velvet dress. Its silver-embroidered hem swayed above her head. "This one's for tonight, for the banquet!" she told me.

"Maureen wore that frock herself, her first night here as a girl," Kate said nostalgically. "A grand banquet that was—so grand she saved the dress all these years."

I gave Kate a closer look. She looked to be my mom's age, but she was talking as if she'd attended Gigi's party.

"I was just a child then," Lexie told me, "too young to be allowed to go. But I'll be there tonight, Lil."

Lexie looked sixteen, at the oldest. "When, exactly, was this banquet?" I asked.

Bronwyn calculated. "That would be nearly fifty years ago now." She sighed. "You humans age so quickly. But let's chat after your bath."

I glanced at the tub again. Then I snatched the dress from Lexie and crushed its velvet to my face. The fabric smelled of Gigi. She suddenly seemed so close I almost expected her to walk into the room. When I reopened my eyes, though, I was still alone with three leprechauns.

Rehanging the dress, I walked over to the tub and stepped in, fully clothed. Slumping dejectedly against its curved bottom, I slid down till the water closed over my head.

"You'll want to give that hair some attention," Bronwyn bossed, rapping on the tub's iron side. "There's shampoo on the ledge."

Exhaling a long sigh of bubbles, I surfaced again.

A shelf next to the tub held an assortment of bath products. Their familiar labels seemed out of place there, beamed in from any normal bathroom in America. Filling my hands with shampoo, I forced my fingers through my tangled hair, too worn out to argue.

Surprisingly, my head felt fine, already completely recovered except for its patches of scorched stubble. I scrubbed away, then slid underwater to rinse. When I came back up, I saw that Kate had dragged one of the stools to the tub's end and was standing on its seat gazing down at me.

"I thought that screen was for privacy!" I protested.

"You're dressed, aren't you? Besides, if I give you your privacy, who'll be taking care o' that rat's nest on your head?" She brandished a pair of tiny gold scissors, snipping the air in a way that made me shrink toward the other end of the tub.

"I don't want short hair." Tears welled into my eyes. "I'll look like even *more* of a freak with short hair!"

"I'll do what I can, but some of those places are down to your scalp. You have to compromise, Lil."

Kate pointed at the edge of the tub, an expectant look on her face. I hesitated, then laid my head there. Short of shaving me bald, there wasn't a lot more damage she could do.

"Lexie! Bring us a comb," Kate called. "Now then, Lil. Are you ready?"

The next twenty minutes were a flurry of snipping scissors. Lexie climbed onto the stool with Kate and used a human-sized comb to lift my long snarls, sweeping it along my scalp whichever way Kate said. At first the comb got stuck every inch, but soon it moved so easily I could tell I had no hair left.

Bronwyn climbed up to check progress. "You've got a spot here needs filling in," she told Kate.

Moving near my left ear, Kate snipped repeatedly a few inches from my scalp. I could see her shears from the corner of my eye, cutting empty air.

"Um, Kate," I finally ventured. "Don't you have to put some hair between those blades?"

"I would if I was trying to make it shorter. I thought you wanted me to grow it. Make up your mind, girl!"

I sat up so abruptly I nearly knocked all three off the stool. "Wait! Are you telling me you can cut hair *longer*?"

Kate glanced at her scissors, then back at me, as if I might be trying to trick her. "What good is a pair o' enchanted shears that only cuts things shorter?"

"But . . . then . . . Why didn't you make my hair all long again?" I wailed.

"Well, now, Lil," Bronwyn said. "It's a bit o' magic, not a miracle. Anyway, Kate's finished now, and a fine job too."

Kate beamed. "Shall I fetch the mirror?"

"Maybe later," I said, too depressed to look.

"Out o' that tub, then, and see what we've got for tea," Bronwyn said.

I stood up, streaming water. Lexie dashed down off the stool and came back struggling to see over a folded, human-sized towel in her arms. Alone behind the screen, I took off my wet clothes, dried myself, and wrapped the towel around my body.

The hut's back door had been opened, revealing a wide field of clover ending against a rocky hill. A teapot had appeared on the table with a heaping tray of sandwiches. Despite everything, my stomach growled as I took the only chair. Kate dragged her stool back over, and the leprechauns climbed up to join me.

Bronwyn poured us greenish tea from a teapot twice the size of her head. The three of them slurped from miniature cups as we sat there eyeing each other, equal height for the first time. I felt like I'd been transported back to one of the pretend tea parties I used to give when I was younger, except that instead of my motley assortment of half-bald babies and teddy bears, the other seats at this table were filled with perfect living dolls in seriously collectible outfits.

"Have a sandwich," Bronwyn offered.

I took one off the stack: brown bread, butter, and some sort of wilted green herb. Too hungry to be particular, I stuffed the entire saltine-sized thing into my mouth.

Kate smiled at me over her cup. "It's a little ray o' sunshine having another girl around."

"Yeah, where *are* all the girls?" I asked. "You're totally outnumbered out there."

"That we are, but that's how we like it," Kate said with a wink. "Makes us special, doesn't it?"

"I guess," I said uncertainly.

"We leprechauns live a long time, Lil," Bronwyn explained. "A very long time, indeed, by human standards. If our numbers were equal between the sexes, we'd have overrun you ages ago. But our lasses are born scarcely one to four lads. It's nature's little way o' keeping the folk in check."

"Lexie here hasn't even chosen her first husband yet, let alone increased the clan." Kate poked Lexie in the arm. "Such a shy, delicate blossom," she teased. "Give us a hint, Lexie. There must be some lad you fancy."

Lexie blushed and looked down at the table. "I'll choose when I'm willing," she murmured.

I took another sandwich, preferring not even to think about the subject embarrassing Lexie. Except . . .

"How does a human get leprechaun blood?" I blurted out. Lexie went even redder. Kate laughed merrily.

"Surely you don't need that explained at your age?" Bronwyn asked. "Your mum didn't teach you about birds and bees?"

My cheeks heated up to match Lexie's. "She taught me birds don't do it with bees," I got out.

"Aye, you've caught me there," Bronwyn said.

"Go on," Kate urged. "Tell her!"

"It happened hundreds o' years ago"—Bronwyn poured more tea, settling into her story—"during a Rendezvous, where the clans meet to mix together. A pack o' lads from all five clans had their fill o' clover ale and were racing dogs in the moonlight when they came upon a dance at the edge of a human village. The sight of so many fine single girls all eager to be wooed by young men near drove our poor lads out of their minds. They knew how heavily the odds weighed against them ever having wives o' their own. So in a fit o' drunken inspiration, they trapped a spotted pisky and demanded a wish for its release."

"More heart than smarts," Kate muttered with a roll of her eyes.

Bronwyn sighed and shook her head. "Piskies are a contrary lot, Lil, and spotted piskies are the worst. Anyone with a whit o' sense would sooner ask for a lump on the head than a wish from a spotted pisky. But those lads were in no condition to think things through. They dragged that tetchy pisky right up to the edge o' the dance. 'We wish all these women were o' a size to be our wives!' they said. 'Granted,' said the pisky."

Bronwyn sighed again. "When those young fools picked themselves off the ground, that pisky was long gone and our lads were human size. And that wasn't even the worst o' it—they'd lost their leprechaun strength, were subject to human diseases, and had human life spans too."

"What happened to them?" I asked.

"Most regretted their unlucky wish and lived out their short lives with their brothers," Bronwyn replied, "but a few went ahead and took human wives, living in human villages and never revealing their true nature to anyone for fear o' jeopardizing the clans. In fifty years, they were all dead. But those giants who wed had children, Lil—leplings—and their descendants live on. Like you."

I had no idea what to say to that. I filled the silence by polishing off sandwiches, forcing myself to chew and swallow.

Leprechaun blood!

The mere idea was ridiculous. I wanted to tell them how wrong they were, to recount all the perfectly normal generations of my family. The problem was, my family wasn't that normal.

Rising from the table, I went back to the cupboard.

There were dresses I recognized and ones I didn't. Two nightgowns hung next to a fuzzy bathrobe. There were a few pairs of pants, some button-up blouses, and, at the end of the pole, a belted sweater with pockets I had seen Gigi wear a hundred times. I stroked its sleeve longingly, as if she were still wearing it.

Somewhere in Providence, my mom was either totally worried or truly irate. I was still pretty worried myself. But how could I doubt now that these leprechauns had known Gigi, maybe even better than I'd known her myself? I didn't believe the lepling story, but I was Gigi's granddaughter through and through, and here, in this strange cottage, I felt her presence more intensely than I ever did at home.

How could I go home without learning why?

Taking Gigi's bathrobe off the hanger, I wrapped it around me and let my towel drop, nothing underneath but bare skin and a fancy gold key. I took a few breaths, steeling up my courage. Then I turned back to the tea party.

"This banquet," I said. "When does it start?"

Chapter 5

"Don't be nervous," Bronwyn advised, trying to push me out the cottage door and into the night outside.

"I'm not," I lied, not moving. I was wearing my grandmother's green velvet dress, which had been brushed until it looked new. On my feet, a pair of elaborately decorated silver flats matched the dress's intricate embroidery.

"Cobbled by Horace Green himself!" an awed Lexie had told me, taking the shoes from the cupboard. "How do they feel, Lil?"

They felt like leather, pretty much, which was surprising

considering that they looked like solid silver. The toes were a bit tight for me, but the soles were soft and springy. Having arrived barefoot, I just had to be glad my feet were nearly the same size as Gigi's.

Bronwyn pushed on my calf again. Still I hesitated on the threshold, deeply apprehensive about venturing into whatever came next. My hand sought out the key around my neck, squeezing it for reassurance. *Gigi went to this banquet,* I thought. *I can at least* pretend *to be as brave as she was.*

"Here we go, then," I said at last, stepping into the unknown.

Lexie led the way down deserted streets, carrying a green lantern. Our footsteps echoed off darkened buildings barely taller than my head.

"Where did everyone go?" I asked anxiously.

Kate pointed forward. "Look."

Up where the houses ended, I caught a glimpse of a mammoth crowd, the sky above them lit in an extraordinary way. Floating nearly low enough to touch, brilliant horizontal rainbows of illumination shimmered and flowed like phosphorescence on a night sea.

"Leprechaun lights," Lexie told me proudly.

"Rainbows at night," I breathed. "They're so beautiful!"

Then we cleared the buildings, and the banquet spread before me. Laid out in a darkened field were a few hundred leprechaun-sized tables surrounded by tiny chairs.

Centerpieces of burning candles lit thousands of pointed faces with wide excited eyes.

The crowd caught sight of me. "Lilybet! Lilybet! *Greeeeeeeeen!*"

As I stepped onto the clover, a volley of emerald fireworks exploded overhead, nearly scaring me out of my flats. Green sparks showered down through the swirling rainbows, and I felt my heart rise up, taking courage in the beauty of the moment.

A bagpipe began playing. Bronwyn nudged my leg, urging me forward. At the center of the field, a large wooden platform held a long, almost-human-height table lit by dozens of candles and surrounded by one normal chair and twenty ladder-legged stools. I made my way to the platform, waving self-consciously to the leprechauns who called my name, pretending not to hear the gossip about me as I passed.

"Lil! Lilybet!"

"If she isn't the spitting image of our Maureen . . ."

"Those shoes are Horace Greens!"

"Lil! Lil, over here!"

"Pretty as a picture, she is. No, an *angel.*"

I climbed the steps to the platform in a daze. I had never felt so popular before—or heard a stranger say I was pretty. In the weirdest surroundings of my life, I actually felt kind of . . . normal.

Five older leprechaun women stood waiting beside the long table, wearing robes of green velvet embroidered with silver. Their white-streaked greenish hair was swept up in intricate dos adorned with jewels and feathers. The most elegant woman in the group had hair that was nearly completely white and wore a robe of pure silver. A tiara of gumball-sized emeralds sparkled above matching crinkled eyes.

"The council," Lexie whispered excitedly, trailing at my heels. "And our Mother, Sosanna, chief o' the Clan o' Green."

The chief's emerald eyes met mine. "Welcome, Lilybet," she said. Her voice was strong and clear despite her obvious age. "You are very welcome."

Sosanna raised a hand and a hush fell over the crowd. "Tonight we feast our sister Lilybet," she called out, "on-trial successor to our beloved Maureen. Let the banquet begin!"

A rowdy cheer went up, drowned by the echoing booms of more green fireworks. The members of the council took seats at the table, assisted by sharply dressed male companions who claimed the stools at their sides.

"Sit down, Lilybet! Take a load off!" a familiar voice urged. Balthazar had found his way onto the platform too. His beard was oiled and braided, and fancy medals covered his coat right down to his round belly. He looked so ridiculously full of himself I almost had to laugh. Instead I showed him my back and took the only chair.

Bronwyn sat on the stool beside me. Lexie got my other

side. Installing himself next to Bronwyn—who I was start-ing to think was his girlfriend—Balthazar winked at me. "Brace yourself, Lil. Here comes the cheese!"

Waiters balancing silver platters streamed onto the field. Some made their way to the platform, while dozens more worked the tables below, serving up an assortment of sliced cheeses. A leprechaun with silver pitchers in both hands filled goblets at our table with a nasty-looking green liquid that fizzed up, then skinned over like pond scum. Balthazar drank his down in three gulps and motioned for a refill. The waiter quickly obliged him before reaching toward my goblet.

"I'm sure Lilybet would prefer water," Bronwyn inter-vened.

Flushing, the leprechaun filled my goblet from his other pitcher and continued on his rounds.

"What *is* that stuff?" I asked.

"Clover ale." Bronwyn sipped hers with obvious enjoyment. "You're a bit young yet. I don't believe you'd like it."

That made two of us. I was about to say so when a new waiter offered me cheese from a gleaming silver platter. Its mirror-like surface reflected a sight I'd hoped never to see: me, wearing a haircut so short it could only be called a pixie.

To my amazement, I wasn't hideous.

My hair framed my face in tufts and wisps, curving into long slender points that made my chin seem less sharp. The craziest part was that spiking my hair made my eyes appear closer together. They were still wider than I would have liked, but that whole bug-eyed look? Almost gone.

"You're welcome!" Kate said saucily from a couple of stools away. I grinned with gratitude, unable to believe I was actually happy about having my long hair whacked off.

More waiters made the rounds. Fruit and bread joined the cheese on our plates. The main course was a hot potato casserole with sides of even more cheese, grilled sausages, and stringy stewed greens.

And last but not least came the doughnuts. Bagpipes played again as a new set of waiters walked in balancing trays piled three feet high with an astounding assortment of doughnuts. There were green-frosted rings, long twists sparkling with green sugar, and golden pillows with green custard filling, all stacked up in concentric rings that looked like enormous wedding cakes. The custardy ones were my favorite, the doughnut part light and chewy, the filling flavored with sweet limes.

"Your gran loved those too," Bronwyn told me as I polished off my second one. "We miss her so much."

"Me too."

She reached over to pat my hand. "Well, we have each other now, don't we? And all the years to come, just like Maureen would have wanted."

Instead of feeling sad, I actually felt kind of comforted. At last I wasn't alone in missing Gigi.

"That's assuming you pass your trial, o' course," Kate piped in. "But the way you take after your gran, there's little chance o' anything else."

"About this trial," I said, snagging another doughnut from a passing waiter. "What exactly is it for?"

"What do you mean, girl?" Bronwyn asked. "It's how you become keeper."

"Yes, but what does a keeper do?"

"She keeps, o' course! She keeps for the clan."

Her answers weren't remotely helpful, but I'd suddenly thought of a more important question. "Bronwyn, if I pass the test, will I be allowed to go home? Balthazar said Gigi came and went as she pleased."

"Aye, and she did, once she was keeper. You'll—"

Bagpipes launched into a crazed fanfare. Bronwyn stiffened with excitement. "Hush!" she whispered. "It's time!"

Across the table from me, Sosanna stood on her stool to address the gathering. "Over the centuries," the chief intoned, "leplings have assisted their leprechaun brethren with many tasks: securing the deeds to our real estate, communications over the water, driving. But for the past three hundred years, ever since Donal Green devised his security spells, having a lepling keeper has been absolutely necessary. May Lilybet Green serve us well and faithfully, keeping the count, transferring what's needed, protecting and increasing the hoard o' Green for the rest o' her natural life."

The rest of my natural life? I didn't like the sound of that. And then things got worse.

The chief raised both hands above her head, palms out toward the crowd. "Let the first test begin!"

"What!" I cried into a deafening roar of approval. "The *first* test?"

Nobody heard me.

I looked over at a grinning Balthazar. "You said there was *one* test!"

"Cheers, Lil!" he yelled back, applauding as if he couldn't understand me over the noise. "You'll do grand!"

Everyone was clapping away as if I ought to be delighted. I shot wounded looks at Bronwyn and Lexie, feeling totally betrayed. I didn't want to take their stupid first test. I didn't want to take *any* test.

I just wanted to go home.

No one cared what I wanted, though. The leprechauns marched me off the platform and back through the town, me protesting the entire way that I was tired, that it was dark, that my stomach ached, all to no avail. Skirting the keeper's cottage, we entered the wide field behind it, only a few torches lighting our way to the rocky hill on its other side. A dark slit appeared between boulders. We were headed into another cave.

"Not a chance!" I said, digging in with Gigi's flats. "There's no way I'm going in there!"

"But you have to, Lil," Lexie said. "That's the test."

"Crawling through a dirty cave?" I was about to tell her I'd already been there, done that, when I noticed the odd expression in Lexie's eyes. She was looking up at me as if . . . as if she looked *up* to me. As if I were one of the cool kids. "What kind of stupid test is that?" I stalled.

"The standard first test," Bronwyn replied. "Nothing to trouble the mind o' any true granddaughter o' Maureen's. Now, Lil, in you go."

Lexie was still gazing at me in that hero-worshipping way. One of my shoes inched toward the entrance as if it had a mind of its own. The next thing I knew, I'd stepped inside a completely dark cave.

"You guys!" I complained, turning back toward the entrance. "Bring in some of those torches!"

In almost the same instant, a grinding, crashing thud jolted the earth as something huge fell across the cave entrance, blocking out all but a chink of dark gray sky.

"Help! Cave-in!" I cried, throwing myself up against the darkness. My hands clawed cold, damp stone.

"It's not a cave-in, Lil," Balthazar chirped cheerfully from the other side. "Bit o' a heavy door, that's all."

They had sealed me in on purpose? I wanted to scream with rage, but I was too petrified. Instead, I huddled against the stone, unable to believe how stupid I was.

Balthazar clucked reassuringly through the tiny airhole. "Now then, Lil, nothing to worry about."

And then a second, smaller stone plugged the opening completely.

I sank to my haunches. The darkness was so intense it seemed to have a life of its own. I imagined it breathing against my skin—until I realized something else could be in the cave with me, something that actually breathed.

What if I'm dragon food? In a meadow crawling with leprechauns, anything seemed possible. Squelching a whimper, I pressed my back against the cold stone and strained to hear any sound: a rustle, a slither, the smacking of lips.

Nothing reached my ears but my own strangled breathing. Even the crowd outside had gone completely silent. Eventually, I realized they'd left.

They probably don't want to hear my screams as the flesh is torn off my bones.

Frightened tears slipped down my cheeks, gradually drying into clammy tracks. Nothing crawled out of the darkness. If I wasn't a midnight snack, why was I there? Was I just supposed to stay put all night, freezing my butt off in the dark? Or was something more expected of me?

Wiping my nose on Gigi's sleeve, I stroked the key around my neck. It felt warm beneath my fingers, full of comforting memories. I ran my fingertips up and down it, thinking of Gigi and happier times. The gold grew even warmer. Then slowly, very dimly, the key began to glow.

I blinked a couple of times, not believing my eyes. But the light got even stronger, cranking up until it blazed. I stared at the key in amazement, and then I realized something else: the rock walls of my prison were visible at last.

The space I was trapped in was no bigger than a classroom. I breathed a sigh of relief as my key light reached its far corners; I might be by myself, but at least I was alone.

I ventured farther into the cave, holding the key like a flashlight. The cave's back wall was a sheer stone face ten feet tall. I shuffled toward it, drawn in a way I couldn't explain. My eyes scanned each rocky bump and divot, and that was when I saw it: carved into the wall, right at eye level, was a perfect keyhole.

And there I stood, holding a magical key.

Not stopping to think, I slipped Gigi's key into the rock. It slid in as if greased, disappearing up to its hilt.

The stone wall shimmered, then vanished in a puff of dust. I gasped as a much larger cave was revealed behind it, one loaded to its stalactites with glowing leprechaun gold.

Chapter 6

ALL the blood in my body rushed straight to my head. Gold sparkled and glittered and gleamed until my brain nearly shorted out. For a moment, I just stood there, staring. Then I found my legs again and ran in among the treasure.

There were piles and piles of coins mounded higher than my head—disks like dimes with holes drilled through them, solid rounds the size of coasters, and quarter-sized coins stamped with clovers and crowns. Gold bars the size of erasers, of sticks of butter, of bricks, were stacked in pyramids ten feet high, right up to the ceiling. There were other golden objects too: plump gold eggs, heavy-linked chains, goblets, plates, a human baby shoe. And filling every space between were truckloads of gold nuggets, from lumps smaller than raisins to hunks the size of my fist.

The gold sucked me into its center as if it had its own gravity. Its strange flickering glow filled the cave with light. I waded ankle-deep through nuggets, my hands reaching out first to stroke, then to grab. Snatching handfuls of coins, I tossed them up into the air and watched them rain back down.

"Whoo-hoo!" I shouted, skipping from pile to pile, kicking nuggets about. My shout echoed off the spiky roof and bounced back into untold tons of hoarded leprechaun gold. I finally understood what I was supposed to be keeping.

I was in charge of all this gold!

Darting from side to side, I touched everything within reach and tried to guess what it was all worth. *Millions, for sure,* I thought. *Probably billions!*

I had never much cared about money before, but I suddenly understood why people spent their whole lives chipping through solid rock or standing in freezing streams swirling gravel around a pan. I knew in the deepest part of myself why people fought and died for gold, and even why they killed.

I had gold lust, and I had it bad.

I ran deeper and deeper into the cave. The gold stretched on like a sweet dream. At last the cave's real back wall came into view, and in a cozy open pocket between its smooth stone and the last mounds of gold were a cot, a chair, a stack of empty burlap sacks with green lashing cords, and an antique desk. A lamp burned on the desk beside an open leather-bound book. I moved closer, intrigued.

Cramped rows of green handwriting formed columns stretching halfway down the book's open page. The enormous ledger was jam-packed with strange names, numbers, and dates. With a start, I recognized the tiny writing: Gigi's. Her final three lines read:

Feegan Green +500 dymers 6 August 48
Evan Green +4 gold eggs 13 August 48
Nonny Green -9 deloreans 24 August 48

I flipped backward through the pages. The book's paper was thin as a Bible's, but somehow the writing inked on both sides didn't bleed through. The last number in Gigi's entries ticked gradually backward from forty-eight to one. Instinctively, I understood that the center column kept track of the gold entering and leaving the cave, but I just didn't get those dates. They obviously couldn't stand for 2001 to 2048, and 1901 to 1948 didn't make sense either.

Finally, on a page by itself, I found this:

Here begins the Accounting of Maureen Green
in the first year of her service as
Keeper of the Clan of Green.

The first line of the next page read:

Balthazar Green -500 deloreans 4 April 1

The dates came clear all at once. My grandmother's birthday was March 31. She must have become keeper four days later. That last number didn't stand for a calendar year at all; it marked her years of service.

Flipping back past Gigi's first page, I encountered a new set of entries with dates running up through sixty-three.

Gigi's predecessor! I realized, flipping madly. *Sixty-three years as keeper! Wait, was this Gigi's grandmother?* The name at the start of those entries was Violet Green. A new thought stopped my breath: *Violet must have been, like, my great-great-something!*

Another set of entries appeared before Violet's, and another before that, keeper after keeper stretching back hundreds of years. *Somehow I'm related to all these people,* I thought, awed. I flopped the remaining pages over to see who had started the book. A letter written in the same green ink waited for me between the book's first page and its cover.

75

Dear Lily,

I'd so looked forward to being here with you, sharing the Meadows together as you prepare for your keeper trial. But life doesn't always go as we hope, and you're holding this letter instead of my hand, so something must have carried me off before your thirteenth birthday.

Whatever has happened, please don't be sad. I lived a charmed life, and you were one of the best things in it. Another thing I loved was spending time here, being keeper for my clan. My fondest wish was to pass this honor on to you—and here you are, preparing to take my place. I couldn't be more proud.

Congratulations on passing your first test! Finding this letter means you've opened the inner keep. You must strive to pass the remaining two tests and become our next keeper. As keeper, you'll receive a share of leprechaun luck and a fine salary for life. More importantly, you belong here, Lily. This is your extended family and a place where you'll always be loved.

I don't know what your other two tests

will be. I wouldn't be allowed to tell you how
to pass them if I did. Just remember this:
You're a Green, Lily. You're Green through
and through. The answers are inside you,
and you'll find them when you need them
most.

I wish I had something truly wise to close
with. Instead, I'll have to settle for a few
grandmotherly pointers:

• The only way back is forward.
• Be what you'd become.
• Leprechauns don't swim.
• It never hurts to take a sweater.
• Lying here is A-OK.

Always remember how much I love you. I
believe that you and I will meet again. Until
then, hold your head up and never doubt
for one moment how truly special you are.

With you always,
Gigi

I put down Gigi's letter with shaking hands. Curling up
on the keeper's cot, I inhaled the hint of her perfume that
still clung to its blanket. Gigi had wanted me right where
I was. She had wanted me to pass my tests and take her
place as keeper. It had been important to her, and that

made it important to me. And maybe, when I was keeper, the pain of losing Gigi could finally start to heal.

The lamp on the desk went out by itself. The gold dimmed to a gentle night-light. I stretched out more comfortably on the cot, not sure what was supposed to happen next.

Balthazar probably expects me to yell for him and tell him I passed the test, I thought. I hoped he was driving himself crazy wondering what was taking so long.

He can wait till I'm good and ready, I decided with a yawn. *After everything he's done to me, he deserves to wait all night. Besides, Gigi said lying here is A-OK.*

For the first time since I'd left home, I felt completely safe. It was the oddest thing, but when I shut my eyes, I could hear the gold buzzing, giving off a low faint hum like a distant air conditioner. Except that the inner keep was warm. Surprisingly comfy and warm.

I shouldn't fall asleep. According to Gigi's letter, I still had two more tests to pass, and I knew my mom must be frantic. *If only I could tell her I'm all right!*

But the only way I knew of doing that was to hurry up and become keeper so that I could tell her in person.

I'll just rest five minutes, I promised myself. *Then I'll totally tackle test two.*

An annoying scraping sound wormed into my sleeping brain. Groaning, I rolled over on my cot.

Then I remembered where I was.

The gold still gave off the same low glow, lighting the cave just enough to see. I stumbled through coins and nuggets on my way back to the front, wondering how long I'd been snoozing.

A chink of sunlight greeted me at the tiny airhole Balthazar had plugged the evening before. I realized I'd slept the entire night just as another scrape and a shout of "Heave!" forced the sealing boulder aside and flooded the keep with light.

I blinked painfully in the sudden sunshine. And then I heard the roar. The field between the cottage and the keep was packed with happy Greens, all cheering like maniacs.

Mother Sosanna stepped into the cave, followed by her council. Her tiara of emeralds looked even more spectacular in the sun, lit through all of their facets into the full spectrum of greens. "Congratulations, Lilybet," she said. "You have passed the test of blood. Only someone with both human and leprechaun blood can successfully use the key."

I still wasn't buying the lepling thing, but I did share Gigi's blood and she had used the key. Then something else sank in: "Wait, you have to be human to use the key? That makes me the only one here who can get to the gold!" I said gleefully.

Just outside the cave mouth, Bronwyn cleared her throat. I noticed the offended looks on the faces of the council.

79

"I mean, um, that's the keeper's job," I covered. "Right?"

Sosanna overlooked my gloating. "Indeed. Opening the inner keep, recording the accounts, and storing and removing what is required are all duties reserved for the keeper."

"You mean . . . even once the wall is open, I'm the only one who can take gold out?"

"Out of the *inner* keep, the keep beyond the keyhole. You'll carry what's needed to the outer keep, which is this part of the cave we're standing in now. Our security spells require a leprechaun to carry the gold outside from here. Checks and balances, Lil."

The mountain of treasure behind me gleamed invitingly as beams of sunlight crept toward it. Dashing back on a whim, I helped myself to a nugget the size of a jawbreaker and skipped toward the outer keep with it. An invisible force at the threshold slammed me backward like a bird that had flown into a window, landing my velvet-covered butt up against a pile of coins.

The members of the council strained to keep the smiles off their faces.

Sosanna pointed at my hand. "You're a bit ahead o' yourself, Lilybet. You passed the first test, but you're not keeper yet. You'll need to drop our nugget if you want to join us."

I uncurled my fingers but couldn't let go. I watched the

gold glimmer, part of me, before I finally forced my hand over and let the nugget fall into the pile.

"Good girl," Sosanna said. "Now come along to breakfast and lock the wall behind you."

I stepped cautiously over the invisible line dividing the inner keep from the outer; then I hesitated, not sure how to lock a wall that wasn't there anymore. But the instant I lifted Gigi's key, the magic stone rematerialized in front of me, sealing off the inner keep with a keyhole at eye level.

Feeling unsure and self-conscious, I slid my key into the lock. Something clicked. The keyhole shrank away from me and blended into a shadow.

"Nicely done," said Sosanna. "Let's eat."

The usual ruckus broke out as we entered Green Field, but this time there were cries of "Well done!" and "Good job!" in addition to the howls of *"Greeeeeeeeen!"*

Our long dining table stood ready on the platform, while the tables and chairs in the field below had been replaced by carnival-style stands serving up fruit and doughnuts to the milling crowd. Painted barricades marked off long empty lanes of turf.

Taking my seat at the table, I waited as breakfast was piled on my plate, then turned to Lexie on my right. "What are those runways for?" I asked, pointing down to the grass.

She looked confused. "Do you mean the race course?"

"Race course?" There was scarcely a man in the crowd

who didn't have an ale belly, and the women were all decked out with ribbons and flowers in their hair. "I don't see any runners."

I'd no sooner spoken than a pack of leprechauns on dogs streaked onto the field. They rode bareback, knees tightly pressed to their dogs' shaggy ribs and hands gripping long ears. The crowd rushed the barricades. I recognized Fizz on a mop of a mutt as a hail of coins hit the grass, all flipped out of leprechaun pockets.

"What are they doing?" I asked.

"Wagering," Bronwyn answered from my other side. "Irresponsible fools. They don't have access to their funds yet."

"Here come the archers!" Lexie cried, pointing.

Dogs and riders took positions at the start of the course as a trio of pipers marched onto the field, followed by two dozen leprechauns with bows and quivers slung over green coats like miniature Robin Hoods. I spotted Balthazar puffing along beside a guy with a mustache that hung past his belt.

"What are they going to shoot?" I asked nervously. Their arrows weren't much longer than pencils, but they had wicked-looking barbed tips.

"Why, whatever you choose, Lilybet!" Sosanna answered from across the table. "They've come to compete for the honor of guiding you on your next test."

"Really?" It was a huge relief to know I wouldn't be on my own again—just so long as Balthazar wasn't my guide. "What is my next test anyway?"

"It's traditional to announce the second test after breakfast," Sosanna said. "Only a select few know that secret, and the whole clan is eager to hear it."

"Well . . . can't I be one of the few?"

Bronwyn scowled, but Sosanna smiled indulgently. "I suppose it does no harm. For your second test, Lilybet, you will catch a spotted pisky and require it to give you a wish of your choice."

Lexie gasped, a long, stunned exhalation. Her small pointed face went as white as whipped cream. For a moment, I didn't get why. Then I remembered Bronwyn's story. Things hadn't worked out well for the wishers in the only pisky encounter I knew of.

"Catching a pisky. Isn't that kind of . . . risky?" I asked.

Lexie nodded vehemently.

But Sosanna just smiled. "The test o' cleverness must be a challenge, else nothing has been proven."

Her ladies murmured in gentle agreement, but Lexie looked stupefied. Even Bronwyn could only manage a sickly grin. A knot tied itself in my gut. I'd gotten lucky on my first test, fumbling my way into passing with no clue what I was doing. If I had to prove I was clever . . .

I'm not *clever! Anyone could tell them that!*

I suddenly realized I had no idea what happened if I failed my trial. I got to go home if I passed . . .

But what if I never did?

A gun went off, starting the dogs and my heart both racing.

The only way back is forward. The words flashed into my mind directly from Gigi's letter. They were more than grandmotherly advice—they were a clue! If I wanted to see my mother again, if I wanted my normal life back, I needed to tackle this pisky thing.

And I pretty much had to succeed.

Chapter 7

"On your marks, get set . . . shoot!" I cried, flinging a doughnut hole skyward with all my strength. The tiny pastry sailed out over the racecourse, a doughy blip against blue sky. Eighteen archers, including Balthazar, had already hit five larger targets, and I just wanted the contest to end.

A flurry of tightly grouped arrows raced up from the ground. Before the doughnut hole reached the top of its arc, the lead arrow pierced it dead-center, knocking the target off course a split second before the other barbs arrived.

"Honor mine!" the mustachioed leprechaun cried. "That's my dart!"

His name turned out to be Cain, and after the arrow was confirmed as his, Sosanna announced my second test— catching a spotty pisky—to the rest of the gathering.

The stunned hush that fell over the crowd made me feel even worse. They started cheering a second later, but my confidence was already shattered. *They know I have no chance*, I thought, slumping dejectedly in my chair.

"Do you want to go back to the cottage?" Lexie asked sympathetically.

"Yes. Let's," Bronwyn urged. "We're done here, unless you're not finished eating, Lil?"

I hadn't touched a bite since I'd heard "spotted pisky." I found it hard to believe I would ever be hungry again. Making our excuses to Sosanna and the council, the three of us set off across Green Field, back to the keeper's hut.

"You guys don't have to come in," I said, dragging my flats up the front path. "If I'm not going on this hunt right away, I wouldn't mind hanging out for a while."

I'd meant hanging out *alone*, but Bronwyn took no notice. "Don't be silly," she said. "I've ordered you a bath, Lexie and I are going to brush up that dress you're wearing, and then we'll all have some nice sandwiches."

"Sandwiches?" I groaned. "I just said I'm not hungry!"

"You're not setting off on a pisky hunt with an empty stomach," Bronwyn told me.

I let them into the cottage, too depressed to argue. The bathtub was already full of clove-scented water. I moved toward it, then stopped. "What happens if I fail?" I blurted out. "If I don't make keeper, then what?"

Bronwyn and Lexie exchanged uneasy looks.

"You won't fail," Bronwyn said. "Maureen sailed through her trial, and aren't you her granddaughter?"

"But if I do," I insisted. "You said yourself that piskies are dangerous."

Lexie stared at the floor, avoiding my gaze.

Bronwyn clucked and shook her head. "That they are. Nasty creatures. Trapping them has been off-limits since the changeling tragedy. I'll admit it makes me wonder what the council is about. But Sosanna is wiser than all three o' us—wouldn't be chief if she weren't. Keep your wits together and you'll be fine."

"But what if I can't catch one? Or it tricks me like it did those leprechauns at the dance?"

Bronwyn hesitated, then sighed. "If you fail, the clan will be forced to take back its key and choose a new candidate. Your memory will be wiped o' all things pertaining to the folk. And we will have to send you away. But it would break our hearts to do it, Lil, and there's no good reason it should come to that."

"Wait, you'll send me away? Where?" Because if they were going to send me home, failing to catch a pisky wasn't just a possibility. It was my new game plan.

Bronwyn shook her head. "No Green has failed her trial in three hundred years, and you mustn't think o' it either. The very shame! Our poor Maureen would never rest in peace again. Not that you'd know how you'd let her down."

"But if . . . wait. Why wouldn't I know that?"

"The memory wipe, o' course! Can't send you back knowing Maureen was our keeper or that you have leprechaun blood, or anything else to do with the folk. You might figure out how to come back and steal our gold."

I rubbed my aching temples. "Let me get this straight. You're saying if I fail, you'll send me home, but I won't remember anything about you guys or that Gigi was your keeper?"

"No," Bronwyn corrected. "You won't remember Gigi. Part o' the folk, wasn't she?"

"You can't do that!"

"It doesn't hurt, Lil. You just drink a little clover tea brewed with enchanted gold dust. The gold absorbs the right memories and passes straight out o' your body."

"I don't care if it *hurts*—Gigi was my grandmother! I *have* to remember her!"

"And you will, because you'll succeed. It's bad luck thinking anything else, and you'll be wanting your luck about you tonight when you venture out after that pisky. Now, take off those shoes and let Lexie give them a polish."

Stepping sullenly out of the silver flats, I kicked them in Lexie's direction. They didn't even look dirty, which was kind of odd, considering all the dirt, grass, and clover they'd stomped through. Taking a seat at the table, I slouched down till my chin touched wood.

Bronwyn climbed up a stool to join me. "Lexie, dear, go fetch the sandwiches," she ordered. "I'm not sure how much longer our Lil will be awake."

Lexie put down the shoe she was polishing and scrambled out the front door.

"So, exactly how am I supposed to catch this pisky?" I asked Bronwyn. "Don't tell me I have to figure that out myself too."

"No, but if I ever had to sleep in the woods overnight, I'd do what any sane leprechaun does—leave out shiny trinkets and clover ale and keep one eye open till morning. If a pisky happens upon you while you're sleeping, your only hope against mischief is a gift it finds acceptable. Piskies are tetchy about their territories, and you don't want to get on one's bad side. Which is why trapping one is . . ." Bronwyn shook off the end of that sentence. "Cain will be there to guide you," she said with forced cheerfulness. "And if ever a leprechaun was born as wily as a pisky, Cain Green is the one."

"He's a good shot anyway," I said, remembering his feat

with the doughnut hole. "I'm not sure about that mustache, though. It makes him look kind of crazy."

Bronwyn smiled. "Crazy when it suits him. Luck was with you when he won the shooting, Lil. If anyone can trap a pisky, it's our Cain."

The sun was low in the cottage's back windows when a violent pounding startled me to my bare feet. I shoved them into Gigi's flats as I ran to open the door. In the closet, I'd found some jeans and a shirt that fit me pretty well. I'd tried on Gigi's sneakers, too, but the silver flats had already stretched to be the most comfortable shoes there.

Cain was waiting on the doorstep, a knapsack slung over one shoulder and his bow and quiver on the other. "Well, then," he said, hiking up a belt weighed low with leather pouches. "Time to go, isn't it?"

"I guess," I said uneasily. "Except I still don't know where we're going."

"The woods, o' course! That's where piskies live, isn't it?"

I remembered what Bronwyn had said about sleeping in the woods overnight. "We're not sleeping outside, are we? Because I camped out with my mom once, and the ground was all rocky, and a spider bit my eye, and it swelled up till I could barely see."

"By all that glitters, girl!" he exclaimed, hiking up his belt again. "Are you a Green or a grumble?"

"Um . . . huh?"

"Grab your things! Let's get hunting!"

I stared blankly before comprehending that I should have packed a bag. What did a person take on a pisky hunt?

"Just a minute." Leaving Cain at the door, I rushed back into the cottage and grabbed the pillow off the bed. I'd learned at least that much from my previous camping experience.

"I guess we ought to bring some food," I said, glancing around. Bronwyn had cleared the table when she left.

"Got it." Cain patted his knapsack.

I found it hard to believe his little bag held enough for two, but I didn't have a better idea. I stuffed some candles and matches into the pillow's case, then dropped the comb in, too, even though my hair was too short to need it. There just wasn't much to choose from, and I wanted to take *something*.

Cain was halfway down the path, impatient to get going. I started after him, then skidded to a stop, struck by a last-minute inspiration: *It never hurts to take a sweater*.

Pulling Gigi's old sweater off its hanger, I shrugged it on and tied its knitted belt. The heavy, cream-colored yarn felt like wearing one of her hugs. Slipping my hands into the deep front pockets, I found a surprise: an unopened roll of Pep-O-Mint Life Savers. "Look!" I sighed with a nostalgic smile.

Gigi had loved peppermint, stashing half-eaten rolls, tins, and bags all over her house. I didn't like the stuff myself, so whenever I'd visited, she'd have a supply of butter rum for me. I would never eat this last peppermint roll, but I'd keep it for its memories of her.

Reassured, I slipped the candy back into my pocket and ran to catch up with Cain.

Chapter 8

"It's getting too dark!" I whined. I hated being so wimpy, but we'd been hiking a couple of hours, and the sun had gone all the way down. Not only that, but Cain walked ridiculously fast for such a short guy. I could barely keep up with him, stumbling over rocks and roots in the dark. "When are we going to stop?"

"Top o' this ridge ought to do it. And by all means, lass, keep to thrashing about like a wounded elephant. Every creature for ten leagues knows we're out here now."

A low-hanging branch slapped me in the face. Shrieking,

I flailed through its foliage until I realized I wasn't actually under attack.

"You *can* take a thing too far," Cain said dryly.

"I can't see! I have to light one of my candles."

"It'll just blow out, won't it? That is, if you don't set the whole woods alight. The moon will be out soon enough."

"How does that help me? I'm going to break a leg *now*."

Cain exhaled impatiently somewhere near my knees. "How do humans get through a day?"

"Mostly in daylight," I retorted.

The woods went totally silent. *Of all the times to think of a comeback!* I berated myself, horrified. *If he gets mad and abandons me here* . . .

And then a hearty laugh boomed out of the darkness. "In daylight, indeed! Well parried, lass."

"So . . . um . . . Should I light that candle?" I ventured.

A green light blazed up on the forest floor. Cain's wide mustache and tall hat were thrown into eerie relief as he straightened up over a miniature camping lantern.

"You had a lantern all this time?" I demanded. "Why didn't you break it out before?"

"The fuel only lasts a wee bit, doesn't it? I was saving it for something important."

"Breaking my neck isn't important?"

Cain gave me a pitying look and struck off through the woods, leaving me to pick up the lantern and follow. He seemed to see fine without it, quickly outstriding its small circle of light while I poked along cautiously behind him.

At first I was glad just to be able to see again. Then the shadows behind every rock, trunk, and branch started looking creepy. They moved with each swing of the lantern, making me even more nervous.

If I do *catch a pisky, I'll wish for it to send me home!* I thought, my first hint of actual enthusiasm for the project encouraging me to walk faster.

Somewhere in the distance, an animal howled. "Cain?" I called, freezing in place. He didn't answer. "Cain!"

Branches stretched toward me like bony fingers. The creature howled again, closer.

"Cain!"

A light winked on up ahead. I sprinted toward it, vaulting rocks and roots, my lantern swinging wildly. In a sheltered nook against a cracked boulder, Cain was building a campfire.

"You're an odd one, aren't you?" he remarked as I collapsed, panting, in the dirt. "I guess it's to be expected. Most initiates come to trial with the old keeper to guide them. You're having to learn it all the hard way."

"Yes!" I said, amazed that the only one who got it was the dude with the Yosemite Sam 'stache. "Everyone expects me to know everything and no one tells me squat!"

"Well, you're lucky I won the shooting today, because

catching a spotted pisky is no small thing. I'm one o' very few living who knows how it's done."

Relief swelled my lungs. "You do? Have you done it before?"

"Well now, not exactly. Bit illegal, isn't it? But tales get passed down over ale—and I've been listening my whole life. Piskies have wild magic, Lil, magic that gets a body's attention."

"Aren't leprechauns magical too?"

Cain sighed. "Not all o' us. Scarce one or two in a generation is born with the touch, and usually only enough to handle a magic mirror or a tricky bit o' cobbling. Master cobblers, leprechauns are, but the last great magician was Donal Green. Ach, he was a mighty one, Lil—created the keeps and security spells for all five clans. But even Donal was no match for a pisky. Leprechaun magic, see, it's all connected to gold. Only gold bows to our bidding. But piskies! Aside from not being able to break existing spells, their magic is wicked strong. Strong and dangerous."

I couldn't say I found that reassuring. "So why are you helping me? I don't have much choice, but you didn't have to sign up for this."

"Plenty o' honor to be had, isn't there? Plus, if you succeed, you'll be keeper. That's a powerful position, lass. Lots o' gold involved." I couldn't tell if the glint in his eyes was firelight or gold lust. "I'll help you now, and you'll owe me later."

"Owe you what?" I asked warily.

Spreading his hands, Cain smiled sheepishly. "Can it hurt to have friends in high places, Lil? A body can't have too many friends."

"Right." Not that I'd know that personally. "So how do we catch this pisky?"

Cain opened his knapsack and took out five small bottles. Uncorking one for himself, he offered another to me. "Clover ale? Three should be enough."

"I'll pass."

With a shrug, Cain opened a pouch on his belt and removed a thin coin with a hole through its center. Gold glinted in the firelight as he flipped it over the flames to me. "There's a dymer," he said. "Piskies crave our shiny things even more than our ale. I've got some buttons too."

Plunging his hand into a different pouch, Cain brought out a handful of the ornate silver buttons the leprechauns wore on their coats. "Can't understand for the life o' me why a creature would choose silver over gold, but these are piskies we're talking about. Their magic may be fearsome, but nobody said they were smart." He handed me the silver. "Place this bait around, right? Make it look tempting-like."

I used the little lantern to find good spots for the buttons—one on a rock, two on a log, one balanced in the crook of a tree—before something occurred to me: "If piskies have so much magic, why do they care about stealing buttons? Can't they just conjure up whatever they want?"

"For all I know, they can, Lil. But piskies never use magic for themselves—some sort o' code they have. Folk say that's what makes them so tetchy when they have to grant a wish. Now hurry up with that bait."

At Cain's suggestion, I set the dymer on a rock by the fire, where it reflected the flames in an eye-catching way. I placed the bottles of clover ale at the corners of our campsite.

"Now what?" I asked.

"Now we lie down and wait, don't we? If you're meant to be keeper, a pisky will show."

"Okay, but . . . When it does, how do I catch it?"

Cain gave me an incredulous look, then burst out laughing again. "By gold and by glory, girl! You've got two hands, don't you?"

"I'm just supposed to grab it? I thought we were using a trap!"

His eyebrows drew together like a second, smaller mustache. "A *trap*? You're going to ask this pisky for a wish, lass. How angry do you want to make it?"

"Yes, but . . ." I flexed my empty hands in the firelight. They looked small and helpless. I *knew* they weren't coordinated. "It's just that I'm not very quick. Or strong. Or brave."

"Brave just means doing what you'd rather not. We all get pushed there sometime. Now lie down and pretend to sleep."

Cain stretched out in the dirt. Reluctantly, I did the same on the opposite side of the fire. I had no blanket, but at least I had a pillow. I didn't expect I'd be sleeping anyway. The thought of catching a pisky with my bare hands had me wide awake.

I hope they're slow, I thought, wondering what piskies looked like. *Tinker Bell would be good. All frilly-skirted and sweet, maybe with a cute magic wand.*

I wanted to ask Cain, but he was already passed out on his back, his "pretend" snoring a little too convincing for comfort. The fire gradually died to orange coals. I curled up on my side, eyes fixed on the gold coin, with only Gigi's sweater and adrenaline to keep me from feeling the cold.

Just like Tink, I reassured myself, repeating it over and over. I wondered if Kendall had gone to see that princess movie without me. No way her mother hadn't filled her in on that mess on my front porch, so maybe Lola had given in and gone with her.

It's not like she'll want to see it with me now anyway, I thought miserably. *She's sure to be mad at me for ditching her.* Unless I was totally flattering myself. Kendall probably didn't even miss me.

I missed her, though. And I missed my mom worse. I even missed our creaky rented house and stupid Providence.

Lying in the dirt with two keeper tests still before me, I would have given anything to beam myself home somehow.

Cain snored on, oblivious. A full moon edged into the sky, silvering our campsite like a scene from a black-and-white movie. I could see every lump of gravel, each needle on the nearby pines. Nothing stirred, not even a breeze. As the moon arced slowly overhead, I felt myself losing what little confidence I had.

No pisky is coming, I thought. *For all I know, they don't even exist. This could be some sort of leprechaun snipe hunt.*

Maybe the real test was just whether or not I was brave enough to follow Cain through the dark and sleep in the woods overnight.

I'll bet that's it! I thought. *They were seeing if I'd chicken out!*

I let out a breath I didn't even know I'd been holding. The night seemed suddenly safer and warm. The ground softened beneath me. My breathing slowed and leveled, carrying me right to the verge of sleep.

A tiny cork popped at my back. My eyes jerked instantly open.

A pisky was into the ale.

I held my breath, listening. There was no sound in the forest now, not a crackle, not a whisper.

Then something brushed the back of my neck, a touch so light it was barely more than a shiver down my spine. The next instant, the gold chain suspending my keeper key yanked tight against my throat, pulled hard from behind.

"Hey!" My hands fumbling at the chain, I struggled to keep it from choking me as I staggered to my feet.

I whirled right, then left. I couldn't see anyone behind me, but the pressure on the chain increased. Wings whirred so close I felt their wind on my ears. And then something small pushed on the back of my neck, using it for leverage. Giving up trying to control the chain, I reached around to grab whatever was pulling on it. A creature that felt like a giant moth skittered from under my fingertips and ran up into my hair.

I screamed with fear and revulsion, jolting Cain out of his dreams. "Catch it! Hold it!" he shouted, still barely awake.

Summoning all my willpower, I clapped both hands down on my head, cupping them over the spot the creature had fled. Trapped wings beat frantically against my palms. A tiny body thrashed back and forth like a rabid bat's.

"Eew, eew, *eew!*" I cried, jumping from foot to foot.

"Now, pisky, we caught you fair and square!" Cain bellowed. "Settle yourself and hear our demands!"

There was a split second of calm. Then a set of sharp teeth sank painfully into my thumb.

"Yooowwww!" I howled, nearly letting go.

"Aye, they bite a bit," Cain said.

"You couldn't tell me that *before*?"

Somehow I held on, pushing my hands into a closed trap and bringing them down in front of my face. The pisky inside fluttered crazily, desperate for a way out. My heart was beating as fast as its wings, but there was no backing out now.

"Just calm down," I begged the pisky. "I'm not going to hurt you. I only need to ask for a wish."

The wish! In a sickening rush, I realized I'd been so busy worrying about *catching* a pisky that I'd never worked out what to wish for. My mind raced frantically.

"Tell it your wish!" Cain urged. "Make it do your bidding!"

I couldn't even see the thing. Was I supposed to talk through my hands? Besides, I needed to stall long enough to think of something.

"How does this sound?" I asked the pisky. "I'll open a little hole and you poke your head out, real slow. Don't try to fly off or I'll have to squeeze."

I braced to be bitten again. Nothing happened.

"Okay, here goes," I said, psyching myself up.

I flexed my thumbs slightly, creating the smallest opening I could. A tufty brown head popped out between them, wearing an indignant expression.

"Sorry! I'm so sorry about this!" I said. "I'll only bother you a second."

The pisky stuck out its tongue at me, a rude slash of pink between toffee-colored lips. *So* not Tinker Bell.

"You're a little thief!" Cain accused. "Going after our private things when we left you so much loot."

"And you're a big one," the pisky retorted in a shrill, whistle-y voice. It bared its teeth in Cain's direction, sharp upper and lower canines like twin sets of fangs. Cain was out of reach, though. The only things close enough to chomp were my thumbs, one of which was dripping blood.

"Okay! Let's not argue," I said, intervening quickly.

The pisky glared at me. "Key."

"What?" I suddenly realized the pisky had dropped Gigi's key in our scuffle. It now hung safely down my back, still attached to its gold chain. "What about it?"

"Mine," said the pisky. "Give me."

"Impertinent bit o' sass!" Cain exclaimed. "That's the keeper key o' the Clan o' Green!"

The teeth came out again.

"It belonged to my grandmother," I explained. "That key is the best thing I have of hers. I . . . Go ahead and bite me," I said, resigned. "I can't give it to you."

The pisky's expression turned suddenly sweet. "Pretty wee shiny thing," it wheedled. "You *can* give it to me."

"I really can't. Sorry."

The creature started squirming again, its wings beating against my palms. I straightened my thumbs, pinning its neck to keep it trapped. "Please! I don't want to hurt you. I didn't even want to catch you! But I have to ask for a wish."

"You *owe* her a wish, pisky! Those are the rules," Cain backed me up.

The pisky smiled and sank its fangs into my other thumb.

"Oooowww! You little—"

The creature lifted its head, licking blood from its lips. "What is your wish, Lilybet Green?"

"You . . . How do you know my name?"

Its tongue flicked out and lapped my thumb again. "This blood is straight down Donal's line. Who else could you be?"

"Oh." Also, eew. "Wait, are you saying I'm related to Donal Green? The magician?"

"Obviously. Your wish?"

My wish. I still had no clue. I turned to Cain in a panic.

"A kingdom!" he proposed excitedly. "A castle, crown, and subjects to the very ends o' the earth!"

"That's . . . a lot," I said doubtfully.

The pisky's wings flapped once. It gave me a questioning look that made me even more nervous.

"I just want . . . I mean, I wish . . ." *What?* Catching this pisky had turned out to be the easy part. If I wished for the wrong thing, I could still end up in plenty of trouble.

"A pet dragon! With a saddle!" Cain urged. "They fly and they're fearsome and no one else has one."

"Do dragons actually exist?" I asked.

"We'll find out together, Lil!"

"Um . . . I don't think so." If making any wish was

dangerous, then asking for a dragon had to be a death wish. The saying "Be careful what you wish for" rang through my brain like a ten-bell alarm. Was there anything I could ask for that wouldn't turn around and bite me? Literally?

I just want to go home, I thought for the millionth time, realizing in the same moment that might actually be a safe wish. But what if I wished for home and the pisky sent me back to the keeper's hut? Or sent the whole clan to Providence with me? Would the Greens wipe my memory for trying to escape?

I wish I were Kendall's best friend, I thought, trying that one out. If I asked for that, would the pisky bring Kendall to the Meadows and strand her with me? Or would something horrible, like a car accident, take Lola out of the picture? I didn't like the girl, but I didn't want to kill her.

I wish Gigi were here. But that wish had the potential to turn out worst of all—what if the pisky brought me Gigi's body? *I could wish Gigi and I were together again instead.* Except that then I might end up dead too. Was there any way to twist a wish to make Gigi alive again into something bad? Could the pisky bring her back but make her hate me? Or turn her into a zombie?

Those were all chances I wasn't willing to take.

"Clover ale!" Cain burst out, unable to contain himself. "A river o' ale for the entire Clan o' Green for all eternity! You'll be a *hero,* Lil!"

No, it has to be something smaller, I realized. *Much smaller. Something so insignificant it won't be worth twisting.*

But what?

What would Gigi do?

"I'm waiting," the pisky reminded me, its tiny black eyes boring into mine. Its foot tapped rapidly against my palm.

"For the love o' gold! Make a wish!" Cain cried.

"I wish . . . I wish . . . I wish you would accept all of our silver buttons and my sincere apology," I blurted out in a rush. "Take the gold coin too."

"That is your only wish?" the pisky asked me with a sly smile. "That is what you most truly desire?"

I didn't like the look of that smile. My heart beat like an off-center washing machine, but somehow I stood my ground. "Yes. I wish for *exactly* what I said. No more and no less—just that."

"Lil!" Cain wailed, collapsing with disappointment. He hit the ground hard, his legs stretched stiffly in front of him.

"Very well," said the pisky. "Wish granted."

I cringed fearfully, bracing for some unforeseen side effect. But all I heard was the pisky's small voice: "Release me now, Lilybet."

"Huh? Oh. Right."

I opened my hands into a shelf. The fully revealed pisky stood straddling my palms, skinny arms crossed over a scrawny chest. The creature wore a rough shift of brown leaves. Its twiggy legs ended in clogs made of bark. And sprouting from the pisky's back were wings like a giant moth's, silver-gray, spotted, and glowing in the moonlight.

"Okay," I said. "You're all free."

Now that the wishing was over, the pisky seemed in a better mood. It grinned around its sharp teeth, its pointed face beaming. "A coin and all your silver buttons—pay up." It pointed to Cain's belt. "One of those pouches should hold them." Flying down off my hands, the pisky landed on the rock beside the dymer and waited expectantly.

"Right. Okay," I said. "Cain, give me one of your pouches."

"What?" he objected, finding his voice again. "You never promised it a pouch!"

"I'll get you another one," I growled between clenched teeth. I really didn't want to split hairs with a creature known for its powerful magic and bad attitude.

"How?" he asked. "With what?"

"Just . . ." I glanced at the pisky. "It's only a pouch, Cain! Don't act crazy, okay?"

The pisky looked back and forth between us, tapping one bark clog. Cain sighed, unbuckled his belt, and handed me an empty pouch. Scooting hastily around the campsite, I filled it with the buttons and set it on the rock. The pisky dropped in the gold coin.

"That's a big load," I said. "Are you going to be able to carry all that?"

The pisky gave me a suspicious look. "Lilybet Green, are you trying to go back on your wish?"

"What? No."

"You owe me more silver buttons."

"I don't! I said take them all, and that's all of them."

"Not *all.*" The pisky looked at Cain again.

"Cain, are you hiding more . . . ?" The answer hit me all at once. "Oh."

"What?" he demanded. "I'm not hiding any blessed buttons!"

"Not *hiding* them," I agreed, pointing.

He looked blankly down at his belly before my meaning became clear. "By all that glitters!" he groaned. Pulling a knife from his belt, he began cutting buttons off his coat.

"Sorry, Cain. When I said *all* our silver buttons—"

"Ach, girl, never mind. No one wishes on a pisky without losing something. You did all right, considering. Although why you didn't wish for something worth having . . ."

"I *have* been asked for more," the pisky acknowledged, watching Cain closely. "Not successfully, you understand. But they will ask."

"I'm sorry to have bothered you at all," I said, handing over the extra buttons. "My clan made me do it, as a test for my keeper trial."

The pisky closed the strings at the top of Cain's pouch and gave me an appraising look. "You're a rare one, Lilybet Green.

Rare good sense for a human and more intelligence than a leprechaun ever dreamed of. May you attain your desire."

"Well . . . I . . . thanks."

"Hold out your thumbs."

I hesitated uneasily. My poor thumbs had barely stopped bleeding. But I was too close to passing my second test to chicken out over another nip. Bracing for more pain, I thrust my hands toward the pisky's fangs.

But the pisky didn't bite. Instead, it folded the tips of its wings over its shoulders and waggled them, showering silvery dust onto my punctures. Flecks of silver sparkled on barely congealed blood. And then the blood disappeared, leaving only two tiny scars, shaped like miniature four-leaf clovers and glowing silver in the moonlight.

"Cool!" I breathed. "Thank you."

The pisky grinned, and its teeth appeared somehow less sharp. "I'm off."

The creature's wings began to beat, slowly at first, then faster and faster. Its feet lifted off the rock, but the pouch stayed put. I was sure all that silver weighed too much for it, but the pisky just cranked up its wings to a hummingbird blur. "Pleasure doing business. Luck be with you, Lilybet Green."

Before I could say good-bye, the pisky sped off at hyperspeed, disappearing like a thrown stone.

Chapter 9

I awoke as the sun topped the trees, feeling truly pleased with myself. I had completed a difficult second test and had slept in the woods overnight, all with nothing horrible happening to me. Maybe I was smarter—and braver—than I gave myself credit for.

Cain shared cheese, bread, and water for breakfast, keeping what ale the pisky had left for himself.

"You did grand last night, didn't you?" he said proudly. "But we'll be wanting to keep the fine points to ourselves. Piskies don't like it one bit if you tell how you captured them. We'll tell the clan you caught one, o' course, just not how. Then you'll tell your wish, and I'll be your witness. That's all folk need to know."

I couldn't understand why he didn't want to brag more. Then a slow smile found my face. "So, for example, it would be better if I didn't mention how badly you wanted me to wish for a saddled-up dragon?"

"It were a *pisky,* lass! I got carried away, didn't I?"

"I get it, Cain," I said. "And I owe you."

He chuckled happily, flushed from three bottles of ale. "Nonsense! We're friends now, aren't we? That's reward enough."

We tramped back through the woods in fine moods, Cain's buttonless green coat flapping, my unnaturally spotless silver shoes flashing beams of morning sunshine. I spent the long hike imagining joyous reunions with my mother and Kendall, certain I'd be seeing them soon.

Back in Green Field, news of my pisky success was greeted with deafening enthusiasm. Cain joined us on the dais, bearing witness to my accomplishment and showing off his buttonless coat to laughter from the whole clan. Balthazar was on the platform, too, his sour, envious expression only adding to my pleasure.

Standing tall beneath her emerald tiara, Mother Sosanna addressed the crowd. "The trial is almost complete," she said. "Lilybet lacks only one test—the test of loyalty. To become our next keeper, she must prove her

111

loyalty by stealing a bag o' Scarlet gold from their very keep."

The resulting cheers were late and stunned. I'd obviously just been handed another doozy of an assignment.

"You don't mean actually *stealing*," I said uneasily. "Stealing would be wrong."

The crowd recovered instantly, laughing as if I were hilarious. Mother Sosanna smiled indulgently at my scruples. "Loyalty, Lilybet. You have your test."

I should *have wished for that pisky to send me home!* I thought angrily, rushing down off the pedestal. *I hate these leprechauns! Them* and *their stupid tests!*

"Lil! Wait!" Balthazar called, running along behind me. "You didn't hear the best part: I've been chosen to help you!"

As if I wanted *his* help. That pint-sized piece of work had stolen *me*. Dashing up the path to the keeper's hut, I slammed the door in his face.

"Lil!" he persisted pathetically. "I want to tell you about the Scarlets! And Wee Kylie! You can't just wander into the Hollow and expect them to hand you a bag o' gold."

"Go away, Balty!" I shouted, plugging my ears and la-la-la-ing until he finally gave up and left.

Silence settled over the hut. That was when it occurred to me that it might have been smarter to let Balthazar speak, at least long enough to hear how I was supposed to steal that gold. Listening didn't mean I had to do what he said.

No, wanting to return home with my memory intact covers that.

Dropping into the only chair, I stared at my pisky scars. My triumph of the night before seemed like a distant dream. The scars had already faded so much I could barely even see them. Dropping my hands, I fingered Gigi's key and tried to figure out what to do.

I must have options. Mom says we always have options.

Option One: I could steal that gold—or try to anyway.

Option Two: I could . . . I could . . .

I had squat for Option Two.

A timid knock sounded on the hut door. Sighing, I got up to open it. "I'm warning you, Balthazar," I began.

But Lexie was the leprechaun standing on the mat. "It's only me," she said anxiously.

I waved her inside. At least Lexie could fill me in on what it was I wouldn't be doing. She climbed a ladder-leg stool to join me at the table.

"It's not fair," I complained. "I never asked to come here. No one tells me anything useful. For all I know, the council is making up tests as they go along."

"For all most of us know."

"I never even knew you guys existed! I was perfectly

happy living a normal life in Providence. Well, maybe not *happy*, but—"

"I understand," Lexie said.

"And now I have to steal or they'll erase my own grand-mother!"

"Shameful."

"If I had any . . . Wait, are you agreeing with me?"

Lexie nodded. "I wanted you to come as badly as every-one else, so I guess I'm guilty too. But I didn't expect it to be like *this*, Lil. I can't help thinking if Maureen were here, things would be different."

"I know! Right? At least I'd have some help."

"She wouldn't be allowed to help you—and she'd never cheat. That's not it." Lexie glanced around, then low-ered her voice to a whisper. "It's the tests. They're too hard."

"Um, that's not actually a secret."

She shook her head. "They're supposed to be hard. But yours are dangerous. Something just feels wrong."

I leaned toward her across the table. "Wrong how?"

"Like . . . like . . ." Lexie peered around again, then blurted it out. "Like someone *wants* you to fail!" She clapped a hand over her mouth, horrified to have said it out loud.

I was pretty horrified too.

"Why?" I finally got out. "I thought you guys couldn't get to your gold without me."

114

"Without a keeper," Lexie corrected. "And you're Maureen's rightful successor. But there are other leplings, Lil, ones who could be tried if you fail."

"Yeah, okay, but . . . *why?*" The idea that I wasn't wanted bothered me more than I would have expected—maybe because it felt too much like the real world. "What's the matter with me?"

"Nothing! I like you ever so much and so do Bronwyn and Kate." Lexie shook her head as if to free it from disturbing thoughts. "I'm probably gathering trouble out of sunshine. If the others find out how I'm talking—"

"No one will find out from me."

"It's just that messing with a clan's gold is no joke, Lil! If you do manage to take some and bring it back, you'll have amnesty at the border. But until then . . ." Lexie shuddered. "If you're caught in Scarlet territory with that stolen gold, you'll be imprisoned for life. You might even be killed! Not executed," she added quickly, reading my expression. "But shooting a running thief is considered fair game. They'll aim for your legs, but arrows go astray when archers get excited, and if you manage to steal even a nugget from the Scarlets' keep, their archers will be very excited indeed."

I remembered the contest in the field, the arrows whizzing toward their targets with deadly accuracy. In my mind, the targets became my calves and thighs, pierced to a bloody pulp as I staggered through strange woods with a bag of stolen gold.

"Maybe it's not as bad as we're thinking," I said hopefully. "Being sealed in the keep was scary, but there was no actual danger. The pisky test . . . that *was* risky. But the only real danger there was making a foolish wish."

That, and the biting, I remembered, feeling both thumbs twinge.

"There are always three tests," Lexie told me. "Blood, cleverness, and loyalty. The test of blood is always the ability to use the key, but the other two tests are unique every trial. Changing the tests prevents cheating. It ensures that every new keeper can handle herself and the gold she's entrusted with. But, Lil, new keepers practically always pass. Their clans *want* them to pass."

"So then why are they going so crazy making up impossible tasks for me?"

"Exactly! That's why if Maureen were here, the tests would have to be different. She would never let anyone put you in danger."

A lump formed in my throat. "She's *not* here," I said bitterly.

Lexie hung her head. "I miss her too. She was like a favorite auntie, letting me hang around, pestering her beyond a saint's patience from when I was the bittyest nipper."

It suddenly occurred to me that Lexie had known Gigi

longer than I had. I envisioned the two of them together, having fun without me before I was even born, and felt a hot rush of jealousy. "She was *my* grandmother."

"Aye," Lexie said softly.

"She's practically the only person who ever liked me."

Lexie's hand reached over to curl around my pinky. "That's not true. I like you."

"Yes, but . . ." *But you're a leprechaun,* I nearly said. Then I looked into Lexie's eyes, as widely spaced and brimming with tears as my own, and realized how little that mattered. All of my jealousy vanished. "I like you too," I said.

Lexie brightened instantly. "Maureen was like my auntie, but our ages are more equal, Lil. You and I can be friends—good friends—if you're willing."

"Do you honestly think so? I mean, I'd like to, but . . . we're kind of different."

"It's true you're a monstrously *large* girl," she teased. "But I can overlook that if you can."

"Funny," I said, "coming from a pip-squeak like you."

"Plus, your hair isn't green."

"Which has probably kept me alive. Surviving middle school is hard enough without hair the color of yours."

"I guess we'll do well enough for each other, then."

"Yes," I agreed. "I guess we will."

Lexie let go of my finger and reached into her coat. She brought out a domed gold button, a four-leaf clover

embossed on its shiny face. "This is my best lucky charm.
I want you to have it."

"I can't take that. It's gold! Besides, I don't have a gift
for you."

"Fare well and come back safe, Lilybet. That will be gift
enough."

Chapter 10

My mood when Bronwyn got me out of bed the next morning was anything but cheerful. I took no joy in putting on Gigi's velvet dress, and I sulked at the table while Bronwyn poured tea and arranged a plate of cheese and doughnuts for me. She had come by herself, which made me hope Lexie wasn't in trouble.

"You know what I've been wondering?" I asked, pushing my untouched breakfast away. "Wouldn't it be easier if you guys handled your own gold, without a lepling?"

"Aye," Bronwyn agreed. "But easier to steal as well. Before Donal's security spells, there was constant thieving among the clans. The Scarlets would raid the Greens; the Browns stole from the Blues. Then the Greens would rob the Scarlets, the Blues would get their own back, plus more, and the Blacks would jump in to mediate and take a cut o' it all."

My head ached just trying to keep up. Until that moment, I'd kind of assumed "five clans" was just an expression.

"For the peace o' all the clans," Bronwyn continued, "we needed a safer way to keep our hoards. There was talk for generations o' some sort o' security spell. Every leprechaun with the touch took a crack at one time or another. Wilster Blue came up with a coin that cried like a baby when it left its owner—made it impossible to spend. Bonnie Black conjured a carry charm that meant wearing an enchanted token before you could carry the bag o' gold it was paired to. That was the best protection we had for years, but o' course folk took to stealing the tokens—and when they got lost, a fine mess that was! Even the gold's owner could never pick it up again."

"So did Donal's spell backfire too?" I asked. "The lepling part, I mean. Was that a mistake?"

"Oh no, Lil! That was the point!" Bronwyn pressed her lips together. "I'm not supposed to say more before you're fully keeper. But one o' our memory wipes hasn't failed in five hundred years, so it's hard to see how it hurts."

I tried to smile encouragingly, but my lips stuck on dry teeth. I didn't need to know that last part.

"Donal had a brother, an identical twin named Doral. Those two were tight, Lil. Thick as thieves. But they had different gifts. Doral was daring and reckless; he loved to dance and drink and race fast dogs. Donal was quieter, but he had the touch."

"Did it make Doral jealous?" I asked. "His brother being so much more powerful than he was?"

"But it wasn't that way at all! Doral was a dog skipper very young, and as fearless a racer as ever there was. He commanded plenty o' respect, while Donal labored in obscurity, barely able to rise to a good pair o' shears." Bronwyn shook her head. "The touch is an unstable thing, Lil. Sometimes it shows from the cradle, then fizzles into nothing. More often, it grows with age. In Donal's case, it was grief fueled his magic. Grief pushed him into greatness."

"Grief about what?"

"Why, you already know the tale. Doral was out racing dogs with that poor doomed pack o' lads. He helped trap that spotted pisky. And he made the pisky change. When Donal found out how he'd lost his twin, he was inconsolable. But there's no going back, not with pisky magic."

"So Doral . . . died?"

Bronwyn nodded. "He was one o' the changelings who chose to live with humans—figured he'd already had the bad so he might as well take the good. Went on to have six children before he succumbed. Doral's death made Donal crazy. He vowed all five clans would remember his brother. And it was right about then that his magic took off."

"Wow," I said, feeling sorry for them both. "That's kind of sad, isn't it?"

"Aye, but grief is a funny thing. It can take the best o' us places we never meant to go. Donal became a hermit, locked himself in his workshop for forty-nine years, and when he finally came out, he had a beard down to his feet and that key you're wearing clutched in his hand. Our security spells were Donal's labor o' love for his brother. He made sure Doral was never forgotten by binding his lepling offspring to the piece o' magic leprechauns coveted most. One o' Doral's granddaughters—Donal's grandniece—was the first to wear the key, and it has come straight down to you."

My mind spun with the implications. "So, I'm not actually in *Donal's* line. I'm in Doral's."

"Same thing, Lil. Identical."

But there was something else that didn't make sense, something Cain had alluded to. "The other clans, their keeps, do they all have the same security spells we do?"

"Aye. The very same."

"With lepling keepers too? How did that happen, if Donal made the spell to honor his brother?"

Bronwyn smiled indulgently. "Well now, they paid him, didn't they? Donal was on the mad side all o' his life and powerful as they came, but he was still a leprechaun, Lil—the richest in all five clans before he went to his reward."

"Super," I sighed, sinking low at the table. "Thank you, Great Uncle Donal."

The only way back is forward, I told myself over and over as our dog cart rolled through the Meadows. If I wanted to remember Gigi, go home to my mother, have a chance to make up with Kendall, and live with normal people again, I needed to steal a bag of Scarlet gold. The choice was so far out of my hands that I'd given up caring about right and wrong.

I obviously wasn't making the rules here.

"Hie!" Fizz called, urging the dogs faster. He was driving again, but in place of Caspar, Cain rode the other lead dog, the ends of his long mustache trailing in the wind. Maxwell had been replaced by a leprechaun named Ludlow. And riding in front of me like a bad dream I couldn't wake up from was Balthazar.

Cain had earned the honor of escorting me through his success with the pisky test. Ludlow was some sort of ambassador, along to make sure I didn't commit any major breaches of etiquette in Scarlet country—which was pretty ironic, considering. And Balthazar was obviously there to irritate the heck out of me, although he claimed to be a guard.

"Are you listening, Lil?" he whined for the millionth time. "You're not paying attention to me!"

"What tipped you off?" I asked, gazing pointedly over his head. Somewhere in the rolling green distance was a whole new clan of leprechauns, the hollow where they lived, and the unfamiliar new keep I was supposed to break into. The last thing I wanted to focus on was Balthazar's nonstop yammering.

"I'm trying to school you, Lil! You may have passed your first two tests, but you don't know everything."

"I know I passed them both without any help from you."

Up front, Cain snickered loudly. "That she did, Balty! Lass has you there!" He flashed a grin over his shoulder, but I was the only one who saw it; Ludlow and Balthazar were riding their dogs backward to face me.

"Perhaps I should take over now," Ludlow cut in. He was a little thing, even for a leprechaun, with an extra-tall hat to make up for it. He fixed me with wide, hypnotic eyes. "Now then, Lilybet. The Scarlets aren't our enemies, you understand. More like rivals. Friendly rivals."

"Friendly!" Balthazar humphed. "Maybe until you cross 'em."

"To be sure. But there's a long and celebrated history of thieving for sport among the clans. If Lilybet succeeds, the Scarlets will be certain to embrace the renewed tradition."

"They won't have a choice, will they?" Cain asked.

The first trace of a grin cracked Balthazar's beard. "He has a point, Lil. Make it past the border, and you'll have amnesty. That's a pure fact."

"Your crime will be completely wiped away," Ludlow assured me. "Only the glory will remain."

"Aye, the glory." Balthazar smiled wistfully. "Glory, to be sure! Taking the Scarlets in their own keep . . . Ach, but they're insufferable, Lil! Never showing us Greens due respect. They *might* be grateful for our Donal's contributions, but there you go. That's a Scarlet for you."

Ludlow gave Balthazar an impatient look. "Those old grievances aren't helpful here. The important thing now is Lilybet's test. None of us can help you steal the gold, Lilybet, but I'm here to make sure your introduction to the Scarlets goes smoothly. A *social* call, that's what we're on."

"As if anyone could enjoy associating with the likes o' Scarlets," Balthazar said, rolling his eyes.

"I seem to recall that at the last Rendezvous, you associated with them fine until their clover ale ran out."

Off in the distance, jagged hills filled the horizon. "Those mountains," I interrupted. "Is that where we're going?"

"Near enough," Ludlow replied. "The Hollow lies at their base."

"Soaking up shadows," Balthazar muttered. "Trust the Scarlets to skulk in the dark when they could live out in the light."

Ludlow sighed with annoyance. "Lilybet's best chance is for us to seduce the Scarlets into believing we're no threat. That means being on our best behavior—and keeping our opinions to ourselves. Surely we can *all* understand such simple diplomacy?"

"The lass ought to know what she's up against," Balthazar said stubbornly. "You haven't even touched on Wee Kylie yet."

"I'm not sure how relevant he'll be."

"Relevant!" Balthazar exclaimed. "He's their keeper, isn't he?"

"He's a boy," Ludlow said.

Balthazar shook his head. "Never trust a male keeper. Only the Scarlets would dream o' having one!"

"They found it preferable to switching lines, as you know very well. It could happen to us someday."

"Never!" Balthazar exclaimed. "The very shame!" He gave me another dark look. "Lives with his clan full-time, I've heard. There's something not right about that."

For once I agreed with Balthazar. What kind of loser would want to live with leprechauns full-time?

Ludlow shook his head. "We don't know that for sure. And even if it's true, he's still only a lad. You shouldn't suggest Lilybet is overmatched."

"I'm *not*!" Balthazar tugged on his beard as if he'd like to pull it out. "Just that she needs to be prepared."

"And that's my job," Ludlow said. "You'll confuse poor Lilybet until she doesn't know what to believe."

Lexie's suspicions of the day before rippled through my mind. If someone in the clan wanted me to fail, Balthazar was my prime suspect. He'd been messing with me since the minute we met.

"Whoa! Ho, there!" Fizz called, stopping beneath a shady tree. "Halfway," he announced, jumping down to unbuckle the dogs. "We'll rest the team here a spell before we press on to the Hollow."

"About blessed time." Cain slid bowlegged off his mount like a cowboy too long in the saddle. "My stomach's been growling the best part o' an hour."

I climbed out to stretch my legs as the four of them watered the dogs and laid a picnic under the tree. The hills in the distance looked forbidding, their folds purple with shadows even at midday.

Scarlet territory.

The only way back is forward, I thought again, chewing my lip.

A poke in the calf startled me. "If you're not going to eat that cheese Bronny packed, how about sharing it?" Balthazar asked.

I looked down at his round belly. "If you really think you need it."

"You can never have too much cheese, Lil," he said, completely missing my point.

I gave him the cheese and some doughnuts, too, and wandered off by myself, still not hungry. I hoped for the hundredth time my mother wasn't too worried about me. I hoped there wasn't a reason to be. I fingered Gigi's key, then the tiny gold button Lexie had given me, recalling her anxious expression as she knotted it on a string around my wrist.

Forcing down a shaky breath, I squeezed the button hard. *Be as lucky as she thinks you are*, I willed it silently.

The sun was sinking behind the hills as we crossed the border into Scarlet territory. Boulders sprouted from the ground, forcing the road to wind around them. Even the clover looked different from the brilliant green blankets we'd left behind in the Meadows. Clumps of maroon-tinged leaves turned their faces into the setting sun and their backs toward us.

I heard a far-off rushing of water. Then a voice cried out just a few feet away, startling me nearly out of the cart.

"Oy! Oy! Oy!"

A leprechaun astride a russet dog dashed out from behind a tree to face us down in the road. He wore tight yellow breeches and a bright red coat, a plume of orange hair rising like a flame atop his head.

"Oy!" he cried again. Yanking his dog's ears around, he turned tail and bolted.

Balthazar groaned. "So much for the element o' surprise."

"Let him tell his council we're coming. We have nothing to hide," Ludlow lied, nodding toward some boulders as if to remind us that more sentries could be lurking. I sat taller in the cart, my eyes flicking nervously over each rock, tree, and bush. The lengthening shadows and thickening woods made more hiding places than I could count.

The sound of water grew gradually louder. We emerged from the trees onto a narrow bridge that arced up over a river. I stared down as the dogs pulled our cart across, my heart thumping in time with the wheels rolling over the bridge's rough wooden planks. The river flowed twenty feet below us, its depth impossible to gauge in the failing light.

"I hope this bridge doesn't break," I said.

Shuddering, Balthazar knocked twice on his pilgrim hat. "Don't even think it, Lil."

On the opposite bank of the river, two rows of trees created a gloomy tunnel over our heads. A cobweb broke across my face, trailing sticky wisps to my ears. Whimpering, I flapped my hands around, hoping to fend off any spider that might be attached.

And then we rounded a bend, and the first lights of the Hollow glowed red through a gap in the trees.

We fell silent as our dog cart rolled down the Scarlets' main street. Town houses six leprechaun-stories high crowded in from both sides, nearly every window glowing red. Startled faces peeped at us through the glass, sporting crowns of hair so brilliant they seemed like the source of the light.

A delegation of scarlet-coated leprechauns appeared in the lane and strode out to meet us, red torches hissing.

Fizz pulled the dogs to a stop. One of the Scarlets stepped forward. I braced myself for anything.

"Greetings, brothers!" the Scarlet leader called with a slight, stiff bow. "You are welcome in the Hollow."

Ludlow jumped off his dog and hurried to make his own, much lower bow. "You are gracious, my brothers. We thank you."

Everyone looked at me.

"Allow me to introduce our new keeper, Lilybet Green," Ludlow said, "come to pay her respects to your council."

"Truly!" The Scarlet leader covered his surprise by bowing in my direction. "An honor, Lilybet. I am Beryl Scarlet. You must allow me to escort you to the hall."

"Um . . . okay."

"There will be food there and such poor entertainments as we can provide on short notice. Had you given us time to prepare a banquet—"

"I'm sorry. I—"

"Lilybet was so eager to meet her Scarlet brothers that she wouldn't hear of waiting to send messengers," Ludlow butted in. "She doesn't crave any greater entertainment than meeting your esteemed council and perhaps conversing with her fellow keeper."

So now suddenly I was keeper—or at least Ludlow wanted the Scarlets to think so. He sure wasn't mentioning my third test. Swinging a leg out of the cart, I lurched awkwardly to my feet and smoothed my green dress.

"This way, Lilybet," Beryl said.

Ludlow and I started forward. Balthazar moved to follow us.

"Surely a guard isn't necessary?" Beryl asked suspiciously.

"Surely not," Ludlow agreed with a scowl at Balthazar. The next thing I knew, Beryl and three of his men were escorting me and Ludlow along the main street, while Balthazar, Fizz, and Cain were hustled down a side lane with the cart.

"Where are they going?" I asked anxiously. They could keep Balthazar for all I cared, but those dogs were my ticket home.

"We can't stable dogs in the center o' town." Beryl's expression suggested he might be wondering if I was kind of dumb. "Your companions need quarters backing up to the woods. They'll be comfortable there, I assure you."

I kept my mouth shut as we walked on, determined not to ask more stupid questions. A few long blocks later, the deserted street opened into an enormous cobbled square.

Red lanterns hung from poles around the square's perimeter, and at its center stood a large building with a roof high enough to clear my head. Beryl led us through its open doors into a high-beamed room filled end to end with rows of dining tables. The benches flanking the tables were full of scarlet-coated leprechauns chowing down. Catching sight of me, they froze with forks halfway to their mouths, their amber eyes popping.

On a stage at the end of the hall, five women in red velvet rose to their feet. A crown of enormous rubies rested on their chief's head, and judging by the serene look in her eyes, she'd been warned about us in advance.

"Presenting Lilybet Green!" Beryl announced at the top of his voice. "Fresh keeper o' the Clan o' Green."

"Welcome, Lilybet," the chief said warmly. She seemed more frail than Sosanna, her once-orange hair faded to peach. "I am Mother Talia. You must eat with me and my council."

"Well . . . um . . . ," I mumbled. Ludlow urged me forward with a frantic roll of his eyes. "Thanks."

Four waiters ran out under a human-sized chair as I joined the women on the platform, but the council's dining table was only as high as my shins. The platters laid out there were heaped with juicy red plums, meatballs with red dipping sauces, and pink-iced cookies with red sprinkles. Despite my nervousness, my stomach suddenly reminded me I hadn't eaten all day. I was about to ignore the chair and belly up on the floor when I saw a second chair coming, along with a human-height table and pretty much the last thing I expected: Carrying that furniture was a guy. A *human* guy. A guy who made Byron Berry look like last week's leftovers.

"You're Lilybet Green!" he said, setting down his table for two. "I've already eaten, but I couldn't wait to meet you!"

He was a year or two older than me, with shaggy light brown hair and wide hazel eyes. Perfect dimples in both cheeks framed an easy smile. He wore red drawstring pants, a puffy yellow shirt, and a black vest with silver buttons—and somehow carried that outfit off. "Kylie Scarlet," he said. "Pleased to meet you."

"Kylie?" The guy was pushing six feet tall, his shoulders were broad and strong, and the hand that shook mine was the size of a man's. "*Wee* Kylie?"

Kylie threw back his head and laughed. "They still call me that, do they? You can tell your clan I'm fifteen now—not so wee anymore."

I nodded, dazed. "*Wee* is the last thing I'd call you."

Chapter 11

"**I** can't believe you didn't tell me about Kylie!" I scolded Balthazar. Dinner was over, I'd been shown to a tiny guest room attached to the Scarlets' main hall, and Balthazar was the only leprechaun I hadn't managed to get rid of yet. Even Ludlow had packed it in, off to crash with the rest of the Greens after a hard day's diplomacy.

"I tried!" Balthazar protested. "If that infernal pup of an ambassador hadn't butted in . . . and himself not half my age! The council will hear o' it, I promise you. In the meantime, let's catch up now. What did Wee Kylie tell you at dinner?"

Balthazar and the other Greens had ultimately been seated far from the stage, surrounded by Scarlets. I had barely noticed them, or the Scarlet council either; all my attention had been on Kylie. The boy was gorgeous in a way I'd never seen up close before.

"I'm so glad you've come!" he'd exclaimed, grinning as if we'd been friends for years. "How long are you going to stay? You have to stay at least a week."

"I doubt we'll be here *that* long." But coming from him, it sounded less like the worst idea I'd ever heard.

"You have to let me show you around. Do you like to.walk? Will you hike with me in the morning?" Kylie's dimpled smile had turned sheepish. "Am I already driving you crazy?"

"Not at all." At least, not in the way he'd meant.

"I need to know what you two talked about," Balthazar persisted. "It could be important."

"Just . . . stuff." The less Balthazar knew, the better—not that I had anything gold-related to tell him. "Do you think you could let me sleep now? I'm getting up early to meet Kylie."

"Meeting Wee Kylie!" he exclaimed, dumbfounded. "For what?"

"We're just going to walk around. He wants to show me the Hollow."

"Ach, but, Lil, you're brilliant! Devious, you are!"

"Excuse me?"

"I'll hand it to you," he said, grinning with admiration. "I've had plenty o' concerns about this test. But pretending to *like* Wee Kylie . . . genius!"

"I'm not pretending," I said irritably.

Balthazar winked a wide green eye. "O' course not."

"Whatever," I said, pointing to the exit.

Locking the door behind him, I collapsed on the red-covered bed and thought about Kylie Scarlet.

Maybe I shouldn't trust Kylie, I worried drowsily. If I wanted to succeed, I had to be smart.

What would Gigi do?

She'd trust herself *and she'd pass this test, like she passed all of hers.*

Stealing a bag of gold had to be doable somehow. Even if someone was trying to sabotage me, the council wouldn't have given me an impossible task.

Unless they were all in on it.

I just need to rest for an hour. Then I'll get up and figure it out, I vowed, plunging into sleep.

I awoke to gentle tapping, a noise so faint I barely opened my eyes. My bleary gaze fell on sunlit red curtains.

"Oh no!" I gasped, bolting out of bed.

I had slept the entire night. I'd never even kicked off my shoes, and my velvet dress clung to my legs in sad, snoozed-in wrinkles. "I, uh . . . just a minute!"

Kylie chuckled outside the door. "Just tell me you're still coming."

"Oh. Yeah. I'm totally . . . yeah," I said, dumping out my bag of extra clothes on the floor. I pulled on jeans, a button-down, and Gigi's old sweater in record time, then hurried into the teensy bathroom to brush my teeth. There were dark circles under my eyes, but my hair looked surprisingly perfect, as if maybe Kate's magic scissors had worked more magic than I'd realized. Taking a last deep breath, I opened the door to Kylie.

The sun had only been up a few minutes. The cobblestones of the square were slick with dew, and Kylie's eyes sparkled with amber flecks that were totally mesmerizing. "You didn't forget, did you?" he asked.

"No. It's just . . . Do you always get up this early?"

"I like sunrises. Don't you, Lilybet?"

"I guess. I wish you'd call me Lily."

Kylie smiled. "Is that what your clan calls you?"

"It's what normal people call me. The leprechauns mostly call me Lil."

"That figures. I'm Wee, you're Lil—the folk are always trying to bring us down to their level."

We laughed at exactly the same time. For a moment, it felt as if we were sharing a joke on our keepers. Then I remembered that *we* were the keepers, and there was nothing funny about that.

Kylie led me down a narrow street through town, then turned right toward the hills. "There's a place not far from here where you can see the whole Hollow, a really great view. You don't mind climbing, do you, Lily?"

It was half-past the crack of dawn, I hadn't eaten breakfast, and the grass at the edge of town was soaking my silver shoes. "I don't mind," I said.

Soon the ground got steep, and the grass gave way to woods. Rocks jutted out of the hillside, cracked and fractured by the gnarled roots of ancient trees using them for anchors. Kylie glanced back as the path got tougher. "Just a little farther," he encouraged.

"Piece of cake," I huffed, determined to keep up. He was wearing some clodhopping human-sized leprechaun boots, but my sleek flats matched him step for step, biting in like soccer cleats. I had no idea where my newfound coordination had come from, but I was grateful some had finally shown up, even if only temporarily.

A house-sized outcrop of rock protruded from the hill above us, cleaved down its center as if split by lightning. Kylie led the way up the rubble between its halves. A few feet short of the top, he turned back to offer a hand, pulling me past him in the narrow space.

"This last part goes straight up," he said. "Here, let me give you a boost."

Both sides of the crevice loomed above my head. Curling

my fingers over its stony lips, I used biceps built by a hundred failed kips on the uneven bars and a foot planted firmly on Kylie's thigh to pull myself onto the rock's flat top. Kylie climbed up beside me, and we stood looking down on the Hollow.

From above, the Hollow didn't look scary at all. There were no shadows from that angle. Instead, the climbing sun lit the top of every tree, turning the dense woods below us into a spiky green sea that rippled in the breeze. The Scarlets' town seemed even more miniature from such a height. I could see the main square, rows of houses crowding in on every side, and away past the farthest outskirts, the river.

Throwing my arms wide, I leaned out into space. "I'm the queen of the world!" I shouted.

Kylie grabbed my sweater belt. Turning my head, I flashed him a grin, but he obviously didn't get the joke.

"Lily! Be careful!" he cried, pulling me back against his chest. "You'll fall!"

I laughed. "I'm only doing *Titanic*. It's not like I'm planning to jump."

"*Titanic*?" Kylie let go of my sweater. We took quick steps away from each other, both suddenly realizing how very close we were standing.

"The movie?" I prompted. "Where have you been living? Under a rock?"

"Something like that." Moving carefully to the rock's

139

edge, he motioned for me to sit beside him, our feet dangling in midair. The Hollow spread beneath us, more rugged than the Meadows but just as beautiful in its own way.

"Is it true you never go back?" I asked. "I mean, you could, right?" A cold fear gripped me. "Keepers *are* allowed to leave?"

"Of course," he said, restarting my heart. "It's just that I have nowhere to go."

"Nowhere to . . . what about *home*?"

"This is my home now. My parents . . ." Kylie shook his head, unable to finish that sentence. The heartbroken look he gave me ran chills down my spine. "Anyway, afterward, I bounced around a lot. Different people, different houses, different schools. All I ever wanted was to have a real family again—and now I do."

He forced a cheerful smile, but this time I could see the sadness beneath his dimples. It made me want to reach out to him, to comfort him somehow. I just didn't know how.

"So you . . . what? Ran away from the real world?"

"Pretty much." He shrugged. "Things are better here. I may be only a male keeper, but at least I'm something—and one day I'll show the clans that boys are just as good as girls. I'm happier here. Really!" he added, laughing at my tragic expression. "Anyway, who cares about me? I want to know about you."

"I . . . well . . . There's not much to know." Compared to his, my life suddenly seemed pretty great. "I live in Providence now. California," I tacked on, not sure if that would be clear. "My mom has no idea where I am; she's probably got the National Guard on speed-dial by now. My grandmother, Maureen, was keeper for the Greens before me." Pulling Gigi's key from beneath my shirt, I held it up into the sunlight, its three emeralds catching green fire. "She wore this key all my life and I never even knew why."

"Aye." Kylie hooked a finger under his collar and pulled out a key set with rubies. Except for the contrasting gems, the keys were identical.

"Even our chains are the same!"

He shrugged. "They all do the same thing, so why reinvent the wheel? Or maybe the magic determined the form."

He obviously knew more about magic than I did. I wanted to ask him a million questions, but caution held me back. It just seemed smarter not to reveal my ignorance until after I'd completed my third test.

And then I had a horrible realization: Kylie wouldn't be answering any questions after I stole his gold. He'd probably hate me!

And what if the Scarlets punished him? Would he get kicked out of his clan? Where would he go?

If he gets in trouble, it will be my fault.

"How long have you been keeper?" Kylie asked. "Not long, or we'd have heard of it."

"Oh, I'm not even"—caution jumped in again—"used to being keeper yet." If Ludlow was pretending I was already keeper, I probably should too.

"And your trial, was it hard?" Kylie asked.

"Not really," I lied. "Was yours?"

"Ach!" Kylie groaned. "The worst! What? Why are you laughing?"

"'Ach, aye,'" I imitated. "You talk like a leprechaun!"

He rolled his eyes. "You'll pick it up too," he warned. "You can't help it after a while."

"It's not a big deal." I wanted to tell him it was adorable, but I didn't have the nerve.

He smiled, and the sunlight edging his shaggy hair framed his face like a halo. "Can I tell you a secret?"

I nodded, pushing down the guilt of not sharing mine.

"Beryl and his men were up all night trying to figure out why you're here. Even our council is suspicious of your visit, but I totally understand. It gets weird, doesn't it, being the only human for miles?"

"*So* weird," I agreed.

"It'll be great having a friend so near, and us nearly the same age too. How old *are* you, Lily? Fourteen?"

"Um, just about." Mathematically speaking, that wasn't

a lie, and if I told him I'd just turned thirteen, he might have guessed I wasn't keeper yet.

Worse, he might have thought I was too young for him.

"Are you going home soon?" he asked. "Back to Providence, I mean?"

"The second I can."

Kylie's face fell, then creased with confusion.

"But, you know, not right away," I backtracked. "And not before breakfast, for sure. When do we eat around here?"

Kylie gauged the angle of the sun. "Right about the time we'll get back, I'd say. And wait till you see the feast they're putting on in your honor!"

"Really?"

"Just wait," he promised, pulling me to my feet. "Do you like cheese and doughnuts, Lily?"

"I don't know why we couldn't do this in my room," I complained, swiping at the swarm of gnats dive-bombing my face. "It's way more comfortable there." After getting up so early, hiking for miles, and then stuffing myself with brunch, the last thing I'd needed was another long walk, but Balthazar had insisted we all meet up in the woods behind the Greens' cottage.

"The Scarlets have spies," Cain reminded me, glancing

about as if one might be hiding behind any bush. "Best not to plot in their own hall, isn't it?"

I shot Balthazar an annoyed look. If he had explained it like that, I would have come more willingly. Taking a seat on a mossy rock, I waited for him to get on with it.

He laced his fingers over his round belly. "Lil needs our help," he announced, gazing from Cain to Fizz to Ludlow. "It's our duty as her brothers to make sure she passes this test."

"What?" I objected. "I thought you weren't allowed to help me!"

"Not directly," he admitted. "But there are—"

"Lilybet is right," Ludlow interrupted. "Our interference would only invalidate her test."

Balthazar gave Ludlow a dangerous look. "Heed me now, pup, and believe I'm serious. I've had all the 'diplomacy' I intend to hear from you. I was a guard before you were born, I know things about Scarlets that you've never dreamed, and I know a bitty loophole when one is staring me in the face."

"Loophole?" Fizz was standing on a fallen tree, minding the dogs through a gap in the woods, but that got his attention.

It got mine too. "What kind of loophole?"

"Well now, Lil, I'm glad you asked." Reaching into his coat, Balthazar pulled out a handful of fine gold chain wound up like a ball of yarn.

"Binding gold!" Ludlow gasped.

Cain gave one end of his 'stache an uncertain twist. "Bit o' a stretch, isn't it? What are you brewing, Balty?"

"We can't help Lil break into the keep. But we can help her with Wee Kylie."

A slow, appreciative smile crinkled Cain's green eyes. Ludlow swayed in his boots as if he might pass out.

I stood up and glared. "Are you saying you want to tie up Kylie with binding gold?"

"Brilliant, yes?" Balthazar asked smugly.

"No! You're not using that stuff on Kylie! *You're* not going anywhere near him!"

"Praises be!" Ludlow exclaimed. "The lass has more sense than her advisors."

"Come up with another plan," I demanded.

"We could try luring him off," Cain suggested. "Did he show you where his keep is, Lil?"

"Of course not." And if he had, I wouldn't have shared that information in front of Balthazar. "Besides, even if I knew where the keep was and Kylie wasn't around to stop me, how am I supposed to get inside? How am I supposed to carry out gold when I'm not even keeper yet? You guys want to help me? How about some help with *that*?"

Fizz met my challenging gaze with an apologetic shrug. "I'm a dog skipper, Lil. If dogs come into it, I'm your lad. Otherwise, I'm afraid I'm not much use."

At least he admitted it. I turned my glare on Ludlow.

"One thing I *can* say," Ludlow offered, squirming, "is that once the stolen gold is in your hands, you've passed the test and become our keeper. We'll celebrate formally later, of course, but you'll be able to exit the inner keep with your prize."

"And in?" I asked Balthazar. "How am I supposed to get in?"

"Well now, Lil, let's work this problem together, one step at a time. No point rushing, is there?"

"That's the first sensible thing you've said," Ludlow told him. "My advice is to do nothing at all for the first month. Lull the Scarlets into a false sense of security."

"Are you crazy?" I cried. "I can't stay here a *month*!" I turned to Cain, my last hope.

"Be certain the Scarlets are wondering why we've really come," he said. "And they'll wonder harder the longer we stay."

"They *are* wondering," I confirmed. "Kylie told me so."

Balthazar staggered. "What else did Wee Kylie tell you?"

"Just . . . stuff. Nothing I want to share with you."

Balthazar's cheeks flushed purple. For a second, I worried I'd gone too far, that he would retaliate somehow.

Then Cain burst out laughing. "Let the lass do it her own way. It's her test, isn't it?"

"B-b-but—" Balthazar sputtered.

"Can't force ourselves where we're not wanted, can we? Just remember, Lil: we're here when you need us."

At that moment, I couldn't imagine ever needing any of them. Not one of them had had a single useful suggestion. Tossing my head in frustration, I stalked off into the woods.

"Lil! Come back here!" Balthazar ordered.

I didn't even slow down.

All morning, hanging out with Kylie, I'd managed to keep the real reason for my visit mostly out of my head. But now the enormity of my third test hit me like that whirling house from Kansas, squashing me under its weight.

If I didn't steal the gold, I'd lose my right to be keeper and every memory of Gigi.

If I did steal the gold, I'd be betraying Kylie, a really nice guy I already liked. A really nice guy who—to make things worse—had no place else to go.

And what if I try but the Scarlets catch me?

I didn't even want to think about that.

Chapter 12

I stamped through the woods for a long time, until I was dirty and sweaty and thoroughly lost. I knew I ought to stop, holler for help, and pray one of the Greens had followed me, but I kept on anyway, too upset to admit I'd messed up.

And then I heard the river.

Ha! I thought, feeling vindicated. *I'll just follow the river to the bridge. Then I can take the road back to town.*

No help from leprechauns required.

Pushing my way through a thicket, I headed for the sound of water. The upper edge of the riverbank appeared and then, as visible as a stop sign in his red pants, Kylie. He was throwing stones with his back toward me, unaware of my presence. Sunlight glinted in his light brown hair as he sidearmed a rock into space and watched it fall to a river I was still too far back to see.

My first impulse was to run out to meet him, but I didn't want him to see me all grubby. Before I could lose myself in the trees, Kylie turned and spotted me.

"Lily!" he cried, lighting up. I barely had time to swipe at my face with my sweater before he was two feet away.

"Hi!" he said happily. "What are you doing out here?"

"Just . . . you know. Walking," I said lamely.

"Walking?" He took a closer look at my face. "Have you been crying?"

"No." I tried and failed to meet his gaze, picturing dirty tracks down my cheeks. "Maybe just a teeny bit."

"But why?" he asked worriedly. "Have we done something wrong? I know your room's a closet, but it practically never gets used. Hey!" he said, grabbing my hands. "How about *I* stay there and you can take my cottage? It has a shower and this great porch swing."

His being so sweet only made me feel worse. I hated the Greens all over again for making me steal from him. My throat tightened over an achy lump. "The room is fine," I forced out.

"Then what's the matter? Tell me."

"I just . . . don't want to be here right now. Not *here*," I added as his face fell. "Just . . . here. You know?"

"Not really. Unless . . . are you feeling homesick, Lily?"

"Yes," I said, latching on to the perfect excuse. "I really miss my mom."

Kylie blinked a couple of times, baffled. "Then just go see her. Go and come back. What could be easier?"

I felt my mouth drop open, trying to catch a good answer, but I had already said too much. With a sick, sinking feeling, I watched understanding dawn in Kylie's wide eyes.

"You can't!" he gasped. "But that doesn't make sense. Not unless . . ." His eyes went even wider. "You're not keeper yet!"

"No! No, I am!" I could tell he knew I was lying. "I mean, *practically*," I amended. "All but the formalities."

"Your ambassador told Beryl you were keeper. You were introduced to the council as keeper! You told me yourself that your trial was easy. Why would you lie to me, Lily?"

"I didn't want to." The way he was looking at me broke my heart. I wanted to tell him I wasn't a bad person, that any lies I had told were not my fault. Except the whole time I was thinking that, my mind was spinning with *new* lies, ones Kylie might believe. Because even though I wanted to, I couldn't tell him the truth. "I can't tell you why. It's kind of a test."

"A test?" Kylie dropped my hands in shock. "Not a *keeper* test? You're here for a keeper test, aren't you?"

I needed to deny it—convincingly and right away—but the woods had started spinning so I could barely stay on my feet. "Kylie," I begged. "Kylie, please. You can't tell."

But of course he was going to tell. He had to. Every single precious memory of Gigi . ... all about to be gone forever. My legs collapsed, dropping me to the clover.

"Lily, relax," he said. "I won't tell."

I hugged my knees to my chest, not daring to believe him. Crouching beside me, Kylie put his arm around my shoulders.

"Lily! Breathe," he directed. "So you haven't passed all your tests yet. So what? Your clan obviously believes you will or they wouldn't have dared pass you off as keeper."

I shook my head. He had no idea what my clan was capable of.

"Come on. Smile!" he pleaded. "I'm not going to tell, okay? If you fail your trial, the Greens will just have to bring in someone else, and not everyone comes to their clans as young as we did, Lily. You're a little funny-looking, but I like you. What if your replacement is some middle-aged nut-job?"

Funny-looking? I lifted a stricken face only to find Kylie grinning. He was teasing me! My heart did this weird, hopeful skip, and even in the middle of that totally called-for meltdown, I couldn't help wondering: was he kidding about liking me too?

"What test are you on?" Kylie asked. "Two? No, wait. It

has to be three. They wouldn't have brought you out here for less than the last one. Right?"

He gazed at me so earnestly, so completely sweet and open and so totally the opposite of the bad things Balthazar had said about him, that my head nodded on its own. As deep as I was already in, it couldn't hurt to admit that much.

"What are you supposed to do?" he asked. "Is it hard? Can I help you?"

"It's hard." And no way could he help. I felt fresh tears rising up my throat. Hunting futilely for a Kleenex, my fingers touched Gigi's Life Savers, making my eyes spill over.

"Ach, Lily. Don't cry," Kylie said. "Let me help you!"

"You can't." Untangling myself from his arm, I struggled to my feet. I needed to get away, to think, to figure out if I had any chance left or if everything was already ruined.

But Kylie jumped up too, grabbing my hands again. "Don't go," he begged. "I'm sorry I was nosy. I was just trying to be a friend."

"I know," I said miserably. I had wanted friends more than anything, and now that I'd finally made one, I had to stab him in the back. "I really need to go."

"Okay," he said, not easing his grip. "But if you change your mind, you'll ask me?"

"I will."

"I'm up for anything," he promised with a conspiratorial wink. "Anything short of a heist on my keep."

My entire body went stiff. What had made him say that? I felt the horrified look on my face.

And then I saw it reach his.

"No way!" he gasped. "Lily! You've come to steal my gold?"

"Not all of it!" I pleaded, the truth tumbling out at last. "I'm only supposed to take one bag and it wasn't my idea! I didn't even want to come here and my clan obviously hates me or why would they give me such impossible tests? I'm really not a bad person, Kylie—I just loved my grandma so much!"

I cried into my dirty hands, too ashamed to meet his eyes. There was no point running away now, nothing left to figure out.

All that was left were the consequences.

"Lily." Kylie's voice was calm and soothing, not filled with the loathing I deserved. "Lily, please stop crying. I might know a way to fix this."

"How?" I sobbed. "Everything is ruined."

"Look at me and I'll tell you."

It took another minute, but I was so desperate to hear his solution that I shut down the waterworks somehow. "Tell me."

"Not here. Let's go talk in the sunshine." Kylie led me out of the trees to the edge of the riverbank. I could finally see the water churning below, but the bridge was lost around a bend. We sat on a patch of clover.

"So here's what I'm thinking," he said. "What if I let you steal that gold?"

"*What?*"

"Shhh!" Kylie hissed, glancing around. "Sentries patrol these woods sometimes. The river covers our voices here, but not if you shout."

I took a couple of deep, calming breaths. "You can't be serious."

"I'm just saying, I *could* let you take a bag. And, honestly, it's probably the only way you'll get one. Stealing out of my keep? Are they kidding?"

I shook my head in disbelief. "Why would you do that?"

"Do you have any idea how much gold is in there?"

My mind pictured the Greens' inner keep—the bars and coins and nuggets stacked up to its stalactites, the twisted piles of treasure, the otherworldly glow of a football field full of gold. My blood tingled at the recollection.

"I have some idea," I said.

"One bag is a drop in that ocean. I can move stuff around to make sure no one notices. And when you're keeper, you'll pay me back. Our accounts will square up and no one gets hurt."

"Really?" I could barely believe he'd be willing to take such a big risk for me. Gratitude welled up where my guilt had been. "You're sure you won't get in trouble?"

154

"Not if you sneak out of here without getting caught. You can't tell your boys how you did it, though. We can never tell *anyone*. If our clans found out, you might not be made keeper, and I don't want to know what would happen to me." Kylie's expression turned doubtful for the first time. "I *can* trust you, Lily?"

"Of course!" I said. "Definitely!"

He grinned. "Then this will be our secret. Swear on it."

"I swear!" I promised. "Totally, totally secret."

"No, silly," he said, laughing. "Clover swear."

Plucking a pair of fat clovers from the bank, Kylie rolled them between his thumb and fingers, squashing them to pulp. "You have to do it too, Lily."

I imitated him as well as I could, until a bit of juicy green squished between my fingers.

"Give me your hand." Kylie's free hand closed around mine. Turning my wrist skyward, he pressed his clover-wet thumb to the pale skin there, leaving a faint green stain.

"Now you," he said, holding his wrist out to me.

I felt his life pump through him as I pressed my thumb to his veins, leaving them smudged with green juice. "Is that all?" My voice sounded far away through the blood pounding in my ears. "You and I have a deal?"

"A clover swear is unbreakable, Lily."

Sudden joy washed through me, a swift, cleansing wave

of relief. I was going to pass my third test! I was going to be the Greens' keeper and go home with my memories intact. Kylie and I were in this together now.

Unbreakable.

I'll prove my loyalty, all right, I thought, *to Kylie and to myself. The rest of the Greens are on their own.*

"So how do you want to do this?" I asked. "Should we meet somewhere secret where you can hand me the gold?"

Kylie laughed. "How is that stealing? You have to make it look good for your clan."

"Showing up with a bag of gold isn't good enough? No one ever said I had to explain how I got it."

"Maybe. But there's still a problem. Leplings can't remove gold from the outer keep. If I ask one of my guards to help me, and then you get caught with that bag . . . You'll have to take it yourself, Lily."

I saw his point. "But if you can't do it without a leprechaun, how will I?"

"You can't. It doesn't have to be a Scarlet, though. One of your Greens can help you."

Great, I thought, groaning silently.

"I suppose it would be too easy if my key opened your keep?"

Kylie smiled, all amber flecks and dimples. "Now *that* I can help you with."

• • •

Darkness fell before I got back to the hall. Balthazar was in a lather by the time I finally showed up. I could tell he was dying to grill me on what I'd been doing all afternoon, but I was eating with the council again and he was stuck at a lower table. Then, immediately after dinner, the Scarlets set off fireworks over the square. The milling crowd, blasts of crimson sparks, and accompanying cheers and applause made conversation impossible.

Knowing the spectacle was in my honor made me feel guilty again, but I forced that feeling down. *I'm going to pay them back,* I vowed, wrapping myself tighter in Gigi's sweater. *They'll never even know a nugget was missing.*

The plan Kylie and I had come up with was foolproof. I just had to carry it out.

A seriously loud finale filled the sky with red and the square with smoke. A row of clover-ale kegs was tapped at the same time, just as Kylie had predicted. In the stampede toward them that followed, I managed to cut Cain from the pack long enough to whisper in his ear. "I need your help with something."

"Aye, lass, that's why I'm here, isn't it?"

"Come to my room at two o'clock this morning. Come alone—do *not* tell *anyone* anything. Okay?"

"No one?" he asked with an eager glint in his eyes.

"No one. Not. Anyone."

Cain grinned delightedly. "It'll be our secret, Lil."

Chapter 13

There was no clock in my room, no way to be sure when two o'clock had come. I'd picked a random time, anyway, just trying to wait long enough for everyone to be asleep—hopefully with plenty of help from the free-flowing ale at the party. Lying on the Scarlets' guest bed with the curtains cracked open, I watched the moon slide across the sky and imagined going home.

My mom was probably really scared about how long I'd been missing, but that would only make her happier once she realized I was safe. She might even be happy enough to throw me a real birthday party. And I wanted a party now, because Kylie had promised to visit me in Providence.

I'll invite Kendall, of course. And Lola too, I decided, imagining boy-crazy Lola's envy when she saw me and Kylie together. *If we hold the party somewhere cool enough, maybe even Ainsley and her friends will come.* Those were the girls I *really* wanted to see me with Kylie—just as soon as we got him some normal clothes.

Or maybe Kylie could come to school one day and walk me home from gymnastics. Everyone would see him then. Except that Kylie might see something too: me, doing gymnastics. *No, the party's a better idea.* Kendall and I would go shopping and find me a new dress, something hot and sophisticated enough to show everyone I'd changed.

They're messing with a different girl, I thought happily. *One with a brand-new boyfriend and a whole new attitude. If I can handle a spotted pisky, I can handle Ainsley Williams!*

Although . . . could I call Kylie my boyfriend when he hadn't kissed me yet? He'd held my hand walking back from the river, and the charge that rushed between us had felt even more electric than a secret cave full of gold. There had been a moment, right before we got to the bridge, when I'd thought he *might* kiss me. But then he'd smiled and dropped my hand.

"We'd better act less friendly for a while," he'd said. "Folk will be watching. In fact, I'll probably ignore you when we get back, but don't take it personally." He'd flexed those perfect dimples. "You and I know better."

My dress for the party should be green, I thought, basking in the recollection. *No, scarlet! Or wait . . . Could I do green and scarlet together without looking like Christmas?*

Something scratched the outside of my door, a long, unexpected rasp that made my blood freeze. I held completely still, then jumped up in a panic. Was it two o'clock already? Belting Gigi's sweater around me, I eased the door open and slipped out to meet Cain.

"Bit late, aren't we?" he whispered, pointing at the moon. His bow and quiver were slung across his back, and his belt hung low with pouches. "I've been skulking about the best part o' an hour."

"Just come on," I whispered. "Quietly!"

We crossed the square as fast as we could, me padding silently in my silver flats, Cain somehow keeping his boots quiet as we blended into the shadows of the first street.

Be asleep. Be asleep. Be asleep, I willed the residents of the buildings we crept past. I could only pray that everyone behind those windows was passed out—or, at the very least, not looking outside.

We reached the woods without being spotted. I breathed easier as we lost ourselves in the trees.

"So what's the plan?" Cain piped up. "A little recon, is it?"

I'd chosen Cain because he'd proven his loyalty on the

pisky hunt and because I had to take one of them, but I still didn't intend to tell him more than he needed to know. I had Kylie to protect now too.

"Just follow me," I whispered back. "And keep an eye out for Scarlets!"

The moon lit our way as we hurried between trees and bushes. I kept to the path Kylie had described, looking for a single enormous pine tree and mentally rehearsing our plan.

A sudden flurry in the nearby brush sent my heart into overdrive. I jumped back in terror, barely keeping down a scream. Cain raised his bow and strung an arrow as a big raccoon tumbled out. They faced off, motionless, eye to eye, before the raccoon turned and bolted into the woods.

Cain flashed me a shaky smile. I knew exactly how he felt. *Just stay brave a little longer and you'll be out of here,* I reassured myself. *The only way back is forward.*

We pressed on until I spotted a low ridge sticking out from the base of the mountain, an especially tall pine a long throw from its end. *There it is!* I thought excitedly. *Exactly like Kylie described it!*

My pulse raced as I rushed to the pine's starlit branches and crouched in the shadows beneath them, squinting across the clearing separating the tree from the ridge. I could just make out a jagged slit of a cave notching the ridge's round end—the entrance to the Scarlets' keep.

"By all that glitters!" Cain gasped. "You found it, didn't you?"

I nodded. "But this is as far as you're going."

His 'stache drooped with disappointment.

"For now," I relented. "I need you to be my lookout. When I've got the bag to the outer keep, I'll signal for you to come get it."

"That's more the thing!" Cain said happily. "How will you get in, Lil?"

"I'll explain later." Or not. "Just make sure no one sneaks up on me."

I slipped off before he could argue, leaving him scanning the woods. Hugging the shadows as long as I could, I broke into the clearing on my final dash toward the cave. Moonlight poured down on my head, casting a spiky pixie-topped shadow across the grass. The four-leafed pisky-bite scars on my pumping hands began to glow brightly again. They hadn't faded at all, I realized; they just had to be seen under the moon. Then I plunged through the entrance to Kylie's keep and froze in utter darkness.

A shaft of moonlight fell through the opening, silhouetting the cave's jagged mouth. That gray slit and the dirt at my feet were the only things I could see. Summoning my courage, I grabbed Gigi's key and forced my energy into it.

The key flickered, then glowed, then burst forth with light. The Scarlets' outer keep was larger than the Greens'. Its ceiling was higher too, but I was concentrating on the floor. Inching carefully across the dirt, holding my key like a flashlight, I saw something gleam near the right-hand wall. Kylie had left his keeper key half buried exactly where he'd promised.

My heart skipped as I picked up the ruby-studded key. Its gold chain dangled uselessly, broken at the clasp. Kylie and I had planned that too, to make it seem as if the key had slipped from his neck unnoticed in case someone else found it first. I'd put it back when I'd finished, and he'd retrieve it later.

Letting my own key hang on my neck, I gripped Kylie's in both hands. *Light,* I willed it silently, feeling my first moment of doubt. What if his key wouldn't work for me? What if Kylie was wrong and I had to be a Scarlet to use it? I squeezed the key harder, giving the task my entire focus. *Light, already. Please!*

A low, warm glow filled my hands. Encouraged, I pumped in more energy, ratcheting up the illumination. The false back wall of Kylie's outer keep was thrown into perfect relief. Directly before me, right at eye level, a keyhole emerged from the rock and glinted invitingly.

It's going to work! I thought. I'd have the gold in a minute, relock the keep, and be on my way. Slipping Kylie's key in up to its hilt, I gave it a firm twist.

The key froze in the lock, and my hand stuck to the key.

The cave flooded with light as an earsplitting alarm went off. I struggled frantically, but my fingers were attached to that key as if they'd been superglued. Flopping back and forth like a beached fish, I watched in horror as the skin of my trapped hand turned scarlet from wrist to fingertips.

"No!" I begged. "Cain! Help!" But I knew he couldn't hear me. I couldn't hear myself over that alarm. I panicked, screaming hysterically, totally trapped.

And then, like a lighthouse in a storm, Kylie appeared at the cave mouth. My whole body sagged with relief. "Help!" I cried. "Kylie, I'm stuck!"

He dashed toward me, crossing the keep in a few bounds. Grabbing my free arm, he twisted it behind me, trying to wrench me loose.

"Hurry!" I begged, just as five disheveled Scarlet guards rushed into the keep, skidding to a stunned stop at the sight of me stuck to their magic wall.

"Lilybet Green!" the guard with the bushiest orange beard bellowed. Taking out a gold whistle, he blew it long and hard.

The alarm cut off abruptly. My ears went right on ringing as more guards poured into the cave, some half-dressed, some half-asleep, all shouting at once:

"What's going on?"

"Is the keep breached?"

"By all that glitters!"

"Thief! She's a thief!"

Beryl pushed his way in and joined the guard with the whistle. "What's going on here, Tully?"

"Caught this sneaking Green, Kylie did!" Tully reported. "And herself red-handed too!"

The whole group stared me down as if they'd caught a serial killer. My legs went wobbly. Luckily, Kylie was still behind me, holding me up by one elbow.

"Stand away, Kylie," Beryl ordered. "She's not going anywhere now."

Kylie let go and took a step back, leaving me still glued to the key. My eyes clung to his, begging him to save me.

"What say you, Lilybet Green?" Beryl demanded. "Has our Kylie caught you thieving?"

I opened my mouth, but nothing came out. My throat felt like it was full of cotton balls. The mob of guards surged closer, everyone shouting again.

I had never been more petrified.

Kylie will get me out of this, I reassured myself. *He'll tell his clan it wasn't my fault, that we were going to put the gold back, that this isn't what it looks like.*

Kylie met my pleading gaze. And then he turned and winked at Beryl. The pair exchanged a smug smile that said more than words ever could.

Kylie wouldn't be coming to my rescue.

He had me right where he wanted me.

It was a trick! I realized, horrified. Kylie had never been my friend—"catching" me stealing had been his plan all along. The way he'd just happened to show up at the river, the way he had guessed my designs on his keep so easily . . .

He was spying on me! Or Beryl was. Maybe the two of them had laid this trap together.

And I'd jumped right into it.

"You don't understand!" I yelled at the guards. Panic forced the blood back into my legs, propelling me onto my toes. "You have no idea! I was . . . was . . . was . . ." I wanted to say *framed*, but my lips refused to form the word. A strange taste filled my mouth, as if I'd been chewing on grass.

"You're making a big mistake!" I yelled, trying again. "I wouldn't even be here if—" Every muscle in my body strained to spit out *Kylie*, but I couldn't. Instead, something else bubbled into my mouth. I wiped off my tongue and stared in disbelief: little bits of chewed clover clung to the spit on my fingers.

"She's guilty!" angry voices cried.

"Caught red-handed, she is!"

"Never could trust a Green, not even a lepling!"

"Praises be for Kylie! If not for him, she might have breached our hoard!"

"Ky-lie! Ky-lie! Ky-lie!" they chanted.

Kylie smiled, soaking up their praise. He looked like a genius, the perfect keeper. And I . . .

I looked like toast if I didn't start talking.

"No! No, I had an . . . an . . . an . . ." *Accomplice* wouldn't come out either, just more bits of clover. My eyes cast about desperately and locked on Kylie's again. Still grinning, he bent his arm in front of him and casually pressed his thumb to his wrist.

His meaning hit me like a heavyweight's punch. My legs went to jelly again.

A clover swear was more binding than I'd ever dreamed.

Chapter 14

"Lil!" a familiar voice called. The sound roused me off the cot where I'd been crying. "Lil, how are you faring? I came as soon as they'd let me."

Dawn had begun to seep through the barred slit of my cell window, and I was desperate to see any friendly face—even Balthazar's. Springing to my feet, I bumped my head in the low-ceilinged room. "Balthazar! Help me!"

A Scarlet guard unlocked a barred door barely larger than a cat flap and Balthazar stooped in.

"Get me out of here!" I demanded hysterically. "This is all your fault!"

I hadn't expected him to agree with me, but to my surprise, Balthazar yanked his beard with two clenched fists and burst into noisy tears. "Aye, and you're right!" he blubbered. "I know you're right, Lilybet. I shouldn't have insisted on waiting for you, but how could I have guessed? Only grandchild o' Maureen and straight down my very own line—you *should* have been keeper, and a great one too. But then you didn't want to come and us without a keeper for over a year . . . Well, how did that make me look? It was vanity clouded my judgment. I should have left you where I found you, safe and sound." He wrung his beard like a dish towel. "Can you ever forgive me?"

I sat down hard on the cot, totally unprepared to see him cry. After all, *I* was the one in jail. "Don't you dare go soft on me now," I said. "You have to get me out of this!"

"But Li—Li—Lillllll . . ." He started bawling again, looking so sad and pathetic and wet I nearly lost my mind.

"Balthazar, knock it off! I'm not kidding." Grabbing him by one hand, I yanked him up onto the cot where we could see more eye to eye. "Pull yourself together and tell me how to get out of here."

He honked into a handkerchief with a sound like a sick elephant. Then he wiped his wet face with his wet beard and regarded me miserably. "They've got you red-handed, Lil."

He wasn't wrong about that. My right hand still looked

like I'd dipped it in paint. "Yeah," I said, holding it up. "When does this go away?"

"That depends." Balthazar collapsed cross-legged onto the cot, wailing pitifully. "Oh, Lil! Why didn't you *tell* me what you were planning? I could have *warned* you. I could have *stopped* you! And to think I carried you into this mess myself . . ."

"I told Cain," I said sullenly, not wanting to admit I'd been wrong to cut Balthazar out of the loop. That seemed obvious now, though. He was nearly as distraught as I was.

"But you didn't tell him your *plan,* Lil. You kept him in the *dark.* And once the alarm went off, there was nothing Cain could do but run back and tell the rest o' us."

"And that's another thing! How come none of you told me about that alarm? We don't have one."

"O' course we do, but it only goes off if an outsider tries to use the key. How were we supposed to know you'd got hold o' Kylie's?"

I would have loved to tell him *how* I got Kylie's key, but I'd already learned the hard way that my clover swear made telling impossible. I hadn't even been able to tell anyone I'd *made* a clover swear.

I sighed. "Couldn't you have mentioned the alarm *anyway*?"

"Aye, and by gold I wish I had! I was just following orders, Lil—keeping unnecessary details mum until you passed all your tests. It's always been done that way."

Bronwyn had told me basically the same thing, but she'd been brave enough to break the rule Balthazar had obeyed.

"I didn't want you to know I had the key," I admitted. "Someone in the Greens is trying to sabotage me."

Balthazar's jaw dropped. "Best be careful where you say that, Lil, but I've been thinking the same thing."

"But who?" I asked. "And why? What did *I* do?"

He shook his head. "The only thing I can work out is that someone wants to switch bloodlines, someone powerful."

"Switch bloodlines? Aren't we all Greens?"

"Aye, but some o' us are related more *recently*, if you take my meaning."

I shook my head.

"You and I, we're like first cousins, Lil. Cain too—he's right in our line. Fizz is more like a second cousin. And Ludlow? Kissing cousin, at best."

"Please don't say *kissing*."

Balthazar picked up on my disgust, but not the reason for it. "Aye," he said grimly. "That lad's been nothing but trouble, him and his diplomacy. He's ambitious too. A cold succession could play right into his hands, although he's not nearly powerful enough to have set all this in motion."

"A cold . . . what?"

"Normally, the existing keeper chooses one o' her descendants to try for the key," he explained. "But if ever a keeper dies without a suitable descendant, or if all o' them

171

fail, Donal's spell allows us to swing over to another branch o' the family tree. Or try a boy—which, I have to admit, is looking less daft than it used to."

"You mean you'd choose one of my relatives? Like . . . not my cousin Gen! You leave Gen out of this!"

Balthazar shook his head. "That girl's no Green. On your mother's side, isn't she? No, we'd hold a selection assembly, and the entire clan would have a chance to put a lepling in their line forward. Every Green craves the status and privilege o' being aligned with the keeper."

"So then who do you think is responsible for making my tests so hard? Who even knew what they'd be?"

"Precious few, Lil, and fewer still with that sort o' influence. The council themselves chose your tests. The only other folk in on the secret were their consorts, Bronny (by virtue o' her relation to Mother Sosanna), me (by virtue o' my engagement to Bronny), Maxwell (by virtue o' my big mouth), and probably a few others I don't know about." Balthazar's eyes narrowed. "Ludlow is in Sosanna's line too."

"So you're thinking . . . Sosanna and Ludlow?"

"Shh!" he shushed me frantically. "How could I? And even if I did, I wouldn't say it out loud."

It was all too hard to follow. Considering where I was, I wasn't sure it even mattered. "Well, if you don't get me out of this cell, *someone* is getting their wish."

"Right," he agreed, nodding listlessly. "Getting you out is

the main thing now. If we're lucky enough to take you home, we can worry about the rest then. I'll get to the bottom o' it, Lil. I promise you."

"What do you mean, *if* you take me home?" The word stabbed like an icicle through my heart.

He pointed sadly to my right hand. "Red-handed, Lil. That's a pretty hard spot to get out of. I left Ludlow parleying with their council but—"

"Ludlow!" I exclaimed. "Shouldn't *you* be doing that?"

"I'm not our ambassador, Lil. They won't talk to me."

"You're *my* ambassador—I'm appointing you right now. Go get in there and do something!"

Balthazar stood up and squared his shoulders. He still looked kind of damp, but some pride had returned to his green eyes. I straightened his pilgrim hat for him and brushed the lint off his coat. With a rueful half-smile, he bowed over his boots.

"At your service, Lilybet."

The ceiling of my cell was too low for pacing. Giving up, I crouched on the floor, gazing desperately through the barred cat flap in the direction Balthazar had gone.

There has to be someone on their council who'll listen to reason, I thought. *This whole thing was just a stupid test. A prank, practically. Besides, how can they not know what a two-faced snake Kylie is?*

Not that I'd figured that out myself. I'd been so pathetically eager to believe someone might actually like me that
I'd never seen the real Kylie at all. It made me sick to realize how short I'd sold myself.

A commotion of boots on the hall's wooden floor sent me
scrambling to my feet. I barely had time to brush off my
sweater before Balthazar reappeared at the bars, red-faced
and out of breath.

"I did the best I could," he called. "There's to be a tribunal, Lil. I'm to serve as your lawyer."

"A tribunal?" The human-sized door to my cell opened,
and I was swarmed by guards.

"Now," Balthazar added, wringing his beard.

A horde of serious-looking Scarlets pushed me out the
door and down a corridor. We emerged into the dining hall,
where I was greeted by boos and hisses. It seemed the entire Hollow had turned out to see my trial. Leprechauns
packed the hall so tightly that the tables had been removed
to accommodate the crowd.

On the stage at the room's far end, three women in red
judge's robes sat behind tall lecterns. Cain and Ludlow
stood off to one side, flanked by Scarlet guards. And lurking in a back corner, his face in the shadows, was Kylie.

I felt him watching me as I passed, but I didn't look his
way. Instead I forced my head higher, putting what steel

I could find into my spine as I was heckled from all sides by the spiteful crowd. The roar of their insults rose to the rafters. *We set off fireworks for you!* their accusing eyes said. *We broke out the clover ale, you ungrateful Green loser!*

I desperately wanted to shout explanations to the whole room, but my clover swear wouldn't let me. My only hope now was Balthazar's lawyering abilities.

He hustled up in front of me wearing a seasick look. The judge at the center raised one hand, stopping us in our tracks as twin trumpets blew from both sides of the hall. Silence descended over the crowd.

"Who brings the charges?" the chief judge asked. I recognized her from the Scarlet council, but the other two were strangers.

"I do!" Beryl strutted forward, a ridiculous white wig stuffed down over his orange hair, and read from a scroll in his hands: "Lilybet Green, you are charged with slyful entry to the Scarlet keep and stealing Scarlet gold. How do you answer?"

"*Slyful?*" I replied. "That's not even a word."

"She pleads not guilty," Balthazar answered for me.

"The prosecution calls Tully Scarlet," Beryl announced.

The guard who had blown the whistle at the keep stepped in front of the judges and shot me a dirty look.

"Tully Scarlet," Beryl said, "can you testify that Lilybet Green was in our keep?"

"Aye! That I can." Tully nodded violently. "Saw her with my own peepers."

"And did she have permission to enter?"

"I'd say not!" Tully exclaimed. "We'd have shut off the alarm, wouldn't we? Not that we *would* have given permission. A Green in the Scarlet keep? Shameful! She took advantage o' our condition owing to the party, that's what. But she didn't count on our Kylie being there to catch her."

Beryl bowed to the judges with a smarmy smile. "First count proven," he said.

"Proven?" I protested as the room erupted in applause. I appealed to Balthazar. "What did he just prove?"

"Your Honors!" Balthazar objected. "With respect, I have questions for the witness."

The judges exchanged looks, then nodded. "You may proceed," their leader said.

Balthazar walked closer to Tully. "You say you saw Lilybet Green in the keep?"

"That's right."

"Did anyone else see her?"

"Half the clan saw her!" Tully replied, outraged by Balthazar's suggestion. "If you don't believe me, ask Comyn, or Duncan, or Kale. Ask Kylie. Ask anyone!"

"You will testify, then, that Lilybet Green was plainly seen in your keep by a large number of folk?"

"Aye!" Tully exclaimed.

I fidgeted nervously, not sure how this was helping me.

Balthazar turned to the judges. "I petition the court: in what way is being openly seen slyful?"

I rocked back on my heels, caught off guard by the circle of Balthazar's logic. The gallery was just as stunned, shouting in angry confusion. The head judge beat her gavel to quiet everyone down.

"Your Honors," Beryl objected. "Clearly, Lilybet Green entered the keep without permission. *That* is slyful."

I wanted to shout that I *did* have permission—from Kylie—but all that came out was a grassy burp.

Balthazar turned to me. "Lilybet Green, did you know you needed to ask Tully Scarlet or one of his men for permission to enter their keep?"

"No!" I bellowed. I'd been so sure the word wouldn't come out that I'd put my whole strength into it. But, I suddenly realized, I *hadn't* known I was supposed to ask those specific leprechauns for permission—and nothing about that question was covered by my clover swear.

Balthazar's an evil genius! I thought, feeling my first glimmer of hope since walking into the hall.

He bowed to the judges. "*Not* slyful, Your Honors. First count *dis*proven."

The gallery went crazy again, making so much noise that bailiffs in black vests had to go up and down the aisles shutting everyone up. The judges leaned their heads together and whispered among themselves. I held my breath.

"The first point will attach to the second count," the chief justice finally announced. "On with your case, Prosecutor."

Beryl shot Balthazar a triumphant look.

"What? What does that mean?" I whispered.

"Double or nothing," Balthazar said grimly. "Winner o' the second count takes both."

"Is that even *legal*?"

"The prosecution calls Lilybet Green," Beryl announced loudly.

"What? You can't call me!" I protested. "A person has the right not to testify against herself."

Beryl appealed to the judges. "Your Honors, will the court please instruct my witness to stop talking nonsense?"

"The witness will answer the questions," the chief justice ruled without pausing to blink.

"But—"

"Lilybet Green," Beryl interrupted me. "Will you raise your right hand above your head?"

"No. I won't," I said, shoving both hands deeper into my sweater pockets.

All three judges glared at me. Balthazar poked my calf. "You've no choice, Lil. Go ahead and show them."

Slowly, with extreme reluctance, I slid my right hand out of my pocket and raised it into the air. A collective gasp went up at the sight of my scarlet skin.

"Red-handed!" Beryl crowed. "Second count proven!"

Cheers for him and hisses for me filled the dining hall. The chief justice banged away with her gavel. Stuffing my hands back into my pockets, I begged Balthazar with my eyes to come to my rescue again.

He met my desperate gaze with one of his own. Then he raised his pilgrim hat and waved it wildly, shouting over the crowd. "Point of factual accuracy!" he cried. "If it please the court, F.A.!"

The chief justice looked skeptical. "State your basis."

Balthazar shot me a now-or-never look. "We will concede that Lilybet Green was caught red-handed *trying* to steal Scarlet gold."

The gallery cheered thunderously.

"But!" Balthazar shouted over the din. "*But* she was not successful. There was no stolen gold in her possession. Factual accuracy has not been met. Lilybet Green has been mischarged!"

The galley gasped. Beryl turned pale. Balthazar had obviously scored somehow.

"What? Tell me!" I begged. "What did you just do?"

"Got him on a technicality," Balthazar whispered back.

The judges conferred again. The center one banged her

gavel. "Is the stolen gold in court?" she asked Beryl. "You *did* recover the stolen gold?"

He was totally panicking now. Sweat streamed from under his wig. "Well, um . . ." He looked desperately from Tully to each of his men as if searching for an answer. My heart swelled with hope. There *was* no stolen gold— Balthazar totally had him!

Then Beryl's eyes landed on Kylie. "Yes!" he cried. "Yes, Your Honors! The prosecution calls Kylie Scarlet!"

Hope shriveled as Kylie shuffled forward and stopped a few feet away. I didn't know what he and Beryl were up to, but I knew it wouldn't be good.

"Kylie Scarlet," Beryl said, recovering some of his arrogance, "will you show the court your keeper key?"

Kylie pulled his key over his head and held it up for the whole room to see. The chain had been repaired so perfectly I couldn't tell it had ever been broken.

"When Lilybet Green was caught, she was in possession of this key. What is it made of, Kylie?"

Kylie smiled slightly. "Gold."

"And how did Lilybet get it?"

This ought to be good, I thought, knowing he wouldn't be able to tell them because of the clover swear.

But once again Kylie proved too smart for me.

"I really can't say," he answered. His words were one

hundred percent true, but his tone distinctly implied he didn't *know* how I'd gotten it.

"Did you *give* it to her?" Beryl persisted.

Beryl had to have been in on the plan since before the clover swear to ask such perfect questions, I realized. He'd probably wanted this chance to look the hero as much as Kylie.

"No," Kylie answered innocently.

"Your Honors!" Beryl said triumphantly. "Lilybet Green was caught in possession of the Scarlets' keeper key. The key in question is gold. And it was taken without Kylie's permission, which is to say, stolen. Second count *proven*!"

The resulting applause rocked the hall. The judges began conferring. I turned to Balthazar, praying he had another rabbit to pull out of his pilgrim hat. "Say something!" I begged.

He shook his head apologetically. "Can't see where to go with this one, Lil. You *did* have the key."

"Yes, but it wasn't . . . wasn't . . ." Chewed clover rose into my mouth. Frustrated, I tried to swipe some out to show him, but I couldn't get anything on my fingers, just spit stained a nearly invisible shade of green.

"It was me and . . . and . . . and . . ." I strained to say Kylie's name, to give Balthazar *anything* he could work with. The word wouldn't come out, but Balthazar finally clued in.

"Oh, Lil! You never made a clover swear?"

I tried to nod, but my head wouldn't move. That swear was bulletproof.

The chief justice pounded her podium. Trumpets blared. The bailiffs ran up and down, calling out for order.

"I am ready to rule," the judge announced. "Lilybet Green, you are found guilty of slyful entering and petty theft. I hereby sentence you to five years' confinement."

The gavel that slammed the podium might as well have hit my skull. My body went numb from the neck down. "Five *years*?"

"What a relief!" Balthazar exclaimed triumphantly. "Five years! I've *slept* longer than that!"

The disgruntled crowd obviously agreed with him. They began filing out, muttering about the good old days when thieves were turned loose in the forest and hunted down like deer. The judges climbed off their stools.

"You can't do this!" I screamed, bringing the crowd surging back. "Five years . . . I'll be eighteen! I didn't *do* anything!"

"Lilybet! Lil, calm yourself," Balthazar begged. "Don't make them reconsider. It's a light sentence, the lightest! Five years will pass in—"

"I'll be *eighteen*! Can't you people add? You can't do this! You can't!"

Guards rushed in to tie my legs with binding gold. They

became useless instantly. Golden lassoes flew over my head, pulling me down by my neck.

"Balthazar!" I screamed, but he couldn't hear me anymore, not under the spell of Scarlet binding gold.

"I'll come collect you personally the instant your time is up," he promised. "You won't wait an extra minute."

"I don't want you to collect me! I want to go home *now*!" I crashed to the floor. Scarlets swarmed around me, making their knots tighter.

Balthazar stood beside my head, gazing down with true sympathy. "I'm sorry, Lil. I did my best. If it's any consolation, one day you won't remember any o' this."

Because they're going to erase my memory! I realized. No way were the Greens waiting five years for their new keeper. I began screaming at the top of my lungs. I wasn't just going to jail and losing every memory of Gigi; I was losing five years of my life! I would "wake up" one day like a coma patient and discover I'd completely missed high school and my sweet sixteen and prom and every normal thing about being a teenager—and I wouldn't even remember why!

"You can't do this to me!" But I was no match for so many Scarlets. They picked me up like a rolled carpet and marched me out through the crowd.

Just before the doorway, I found myself looking up at

Kylie. I could guess why he'd done it: no one would ever say boys couldn't be good keepers again. Making it look as if he'd caught me at my own plan made him seem even more clever. But he'd never thought too deeply about what would happen to me—I could read that in his eyes. For a moment, I thought I saw remorse there too.

Then his gaze flicked away.

"Kylie!" I screamed. "Don't let them do this!"

The last thing I saw in that hall was Kylie turning his back on me, abandoning me to my sentence.

Chapter 15

Things went kind of black after that, what with the panic and screaming and all. The next thing I remember is a long blur of branches overhead, then hitting the dirt on my back.

"Get the door," Tully's voice ordered.

My head crunched through fallen leaves as I looked side to side for a building. We were out in the middle of the woods somewhere, not a thing around us but trees, dirt, and boulders the size of minivans.

Hinges squealed.

"Hoist her up and in she goes!"

Hands pushed me back into the air. I saw the short, squeaky door as I was carried past it—a six-inch-thick slab of wood reinforced with iron bars. Daylight gave way to dim shadows. There was stone overhead, stone all around. I hit the ground again, harder. There was stone beneath me too.

"Good enough," a rough voice said. "Lively now, lads."

I felt tugging on the binding gold around my legs and neck. "Crying shame to turn this over to that maggot o' an ambassador," someone said.

"Aye, but what can we do? Council's ruled in the maggot's favor," Tully replied disgustedly.

Hinges squealed and the door slammed. I lay motionless another minute before I realized I'd been untied and all the leprechauns had gone. I was free—free inside a smaller, drearier, even more escape-proof cell than I'd been held in before.

My prison seemed to be a huge, hollowed-out boulder. Chisel marks pocked the curved walls and ceiling, making a rounded space the size of my bathroom at home, only with a lower ceiling. Near the center, I could stand up straight; everywhere else I had to stoop. A ledge along the wall held a moldy mattress. There were two buckets against the opposite wall, one filled with water and an empty one the purpose of which I didn't want to think about.

The only way in or out was through the battering-ram-proof timber door. The single other opening was a hole eighteen inches square, crisscrossed with so many bars I could barely reach my hand out. The stone through which that window had been cut formed a foot-wide ledge in front of the grate. Resting my chin there, I tried to see where I was, but there was nothing I recognized outside, just rocks and trees and a pond so small it looked more like a puddle. I had been carried so far from town I couldn't even guess which direction it was in.

Something clanged loudly behind me. A bag was being shoved through a slot that had opened in the door. Sprawling flat, I peered through the slot before it closed again.

"Help! Stay! Wait!" I cried, startling the leprechaun on the other side into nearly tumbling over. He was too young to grow a beard, and he wore a waiter's apron.

"Don't try anything, Green, or I'll call Tully!" he warned.

"I just want to see Balthazar. Or Cain. When are they coming?"

The waiter collected himself and ventured back to the door. "Here? You're in confinement, aren't you? No visitors."

The slot cover slammed in my face.

"No visitors *when*?" I shouted. "You don't mean ever! No visitors *ever*?"

"No visitors for prisoners in confinement. Everyone knows that."

"No, they don't!" I cried. "No visitors? Are you kidding me?"

No answer came from outside the door. Silence descended over the woods, driving me into a fresh panic.

"Let me out!" I shrieked, charging the window. I scraped my knuckles trying to shake the bars loose, but the iron didn't budge. Screaming until my throat was raw, I collapsed into a hysterical heap on the mattress.

No one is coming to rescue me, I realized.

I was on my own. Abandoned.

For all I knew, the Greens had already left.

I sobbed inconsolably, heartbroken by all I had lost. I had arrived desperately missing Gigi, and in a few years I wouldn't remember her. I couldn't even be certain I'd ever see my mother again; one of us could *die* in five years. I had taken her completely for granted, and now it was too late. Never once had it crossed my mind that I could lose her too.

I huddled tighter in Gigi's sweater. Its yarn was getting grubby, but it was still the most comforting thing there, next to Gigi's key. I reached for that under my collar.

There was no gold chain around my neck.

Bolting upright, I frisked myself, then looked wildly about the cell. Gigi's key was gone.

They took it! I realized. I remembered the tugging around my neck, hearing something about a maggot of an ambassador . . .

Ludlow! I thought, furious. *This was all his doing!*

If my wardens were bringing him my key, though, that meant the Greens were still in the Hollow. And unless Fizz wanted to drive in the dark, they probably wouldn't leave before morning.

Which did me exactly no good at all.

I sank back onto the mattress, watching miserably as a square of light from the window inched slowly across my cell wall. I would never survive five years in this place. I'd lose my mind the first week.

I had to escape.

But how?

It wasn't as if I had much to work with. I took an inventory: one moldy mattress, two buckets, the clothes I was wearing, a pack of peppermint Life Savers, and Lexie's good-luck charm—which obviously hadn't been lucky for me.

How was I supposed to accomplish a jailbreak with that?

Words from Gigi's letter popped into my head: *Be what you'd become.*

Okay, fine. Except that I had no idea what that meant.

I struggled to reason it out: *I want to go home now with my memory intact. That means I have to become keeper. Keepers are clever. I have to be clever.*

Great.

The last thing I felt at that moment was clever, but I forced myself to start trying.

Was there any way I could use Lexie's gold button? Untying it from my wrist, I laid it before me. The belt on Gigi's sweater could serve as a short rope; I put that on the mattress too. Then I took out her Life Savers.

I wish these were butter rum now, I thought, examining the worn foil of the roll's unopened ends. If that was the only candy I'd see for the next five years, it could at least have been one I wanted to eat.

Placing the Life Savers next to the belt, I stared down at my meager tools. Maybe I could tie the belt to the window and use it to pull out the bars?

No way. That yarn will break before those bars ever do.

I got up for another look anyway. The woods outside the window had slipped into twilight and were darkening fast. I longed to lose myself in them, but the iron bars were spaced so tightly that even a leprechaun couldn't slip through. There was barely room for a pisky.

I froze where I stood, struck by a sudden inspiration. Was I completely insane to be thinking what I was thinking?

Do I have any choice?

Chapter 16

This is a stupid idea, I thought. *Give up now and admit it.*

It had to be past midnight, and my legs were so cramped from crouching that I wasn't sure I'd be able to stand, let alone spring up to the window. But I stayed where I was.

I had no Plan B.

Directly above me, on the window ledge, my meager offerings were spread: Lexie's gold charm and four peppermint Life Savers. I'd shredded the foil off the candy's waxed paper and scattered those shiny scraps around too. They glimmered in the moonlight, adding badly needed flash, but I didn't have any real silver, or ale, or anything else that a pisky might like. All I had was hope and my desperation.

A pisky will come, I argued with the part of me that wanted to quit. *Lexie's gold button is worth taking, and I put that right up front.*

My cramped legs began to quiver—I had to stretch them out. Scooting over a few inches, I rose painfully beside the cell window, flattened my back to the wall, and peered out sideways. The sky above the pines was full of stars. Beneath the trees, a pattern of silver and shadow patch-worked the ground like a quilt. I was jiggling blood back into my feet when a blur of wings cut through a moonbeam and a pisky landed on my windowsill.

I went as still as the stone wall. The pisky hesitated, listening, then walked in through the bars, headed for Lexie's button.

Don't move. Don't even breathe! I warned myself. I'd only get one chance.

The pisky bent to pick up the gold.

I pounced.

Launching myself at the ledge, I grabbed for the pisky as if my life depended on it. The startled creature fell backward onto its wings. Before it could flip over to fly, both of my hands clamped down like a dome, trapping it on the ledge.

"Sorry! Sorry!" I cried as it flailed against my palms. "I'm not going to hurt you! I'm really, truly sorry, but I've got to have a wish."

The whirring wings slowed to a flutter. I imagined the pisky baring its fangs, choosing the juiciest spot to sink them. I braced myself to hold on despite any amount of chomping.

And then the pisky started to laugh.

Its reedy giggle filled my hands, my ears, the entire cell. "Release me!" it chirped mirthfully.

I watched in disbelief as my hands peeled away on their own, leaving the pisky completely uncaught. The creature brushed off its skinny arms and wriggled its spotted wings, twitching itself back into position. My hands hovered inches away, but no matter how I tried, I couldn't force them to grab. The scars on my thumbs glowed silver, tiny clovers in the moonlight. The pisky grinned as it pointed them out.

"No double-dipping," it gloated. "You've been marked."

My fingers strained toward the ledge but refused to move.

"Put your arms down," the pisky commanded. They dropped to my sides. "Good girl. Now stay."

Being told to stay made me even more determined to move. I tried to lunge again, only to discover that my feet had stuck to the floor. My shoulders barely twitched. And I couldn't lift my hands. "What have you done to me?" I cried.

"Well now," the pisky said with a smile, "the first time you catch a pisky, we're in your power. The next time, you're in ours. Those chuckleheaded leprechauns didn't tell you that?"

"You wouldn't believe how much they didn't tell me," I answered sullenly.

The pisky smiled and picked up Lexie's button. "I'll be having this, for starters. What did you get off Kinkle?"

"Excuse me?"

Cradling the button in one arm, it pointed toward my right hand. My arm flew up, thumb first, forcing my glowing scar into the moonlight. "That's Kinkle's work, yes?"

"I, um, didn't get a name."

"Well now," the pisky said approvingly, "it isn't polite to ask, is it? But I'd recognize Kinkle's mark anywhere. What did you wish for? Wait, let me guess!" The pisky glanced around my stone cell. "A house no one could break into? A long vacation someplace you wouldn't be bothered?"

"I didn't ask for anything! I only wished that Kinkle would accept our silver buttons and my apologies for bothering, um . . . Kinkle." I wasn't exactly sure if these piskies were boys or girls. "My clan made me do it. All I really wanted was to go home."

The creature gave me a skeptical look. "Then how did you end up here?"

"That's a long, sad story. Hey!" I said, sensing a possible

loophole. "Since making that first wish wasn't my idea, and I didn't get anything out of it, can't—"

"You got those scars," the pisky said. "And from the way they've been silvered, you got off easy. If Kinkle hadn't dusted those bites, they'd have been ugly welts till the day you died. You must have made a good impression."

"Yes!" I said, grasping at that straw. "Kinkle liked me! Let's call Kinkle!"

"Won't change the rules. One wish per customer."

The pisky stooped to push its free hand through the center of one Life Saver, then another, threading them onto its twiggy arm like candy snow tires. Shifting the gold button awkwardly over on top of them, it threaded the remaining two peppermints onto its other arm, clasping its hands in front to hold everything together. The objects made an awkward load—four Life Savers stretching the limits of the pisky's reach, the button balanced on top like a basketball too big to sink.

"I'm not going to be stuck like this forever, am I?" I asked.

The pisky craned its neck around the button to look at me. "That depends. Do you have any silver?"

"No," I said despairingly. "I had a gold key, but they took it."

Hopping from scrap to scrap, the pisky kicked each bit of foil, checking underneath. Its arms were so full it could barely see, peering awkwardly around one elbow. "You don't like to stand still?" it asked. "Would you rather dance?"

"Um . . . well . . ." Was that a trick question? "I'd rather be *able* to dance. And stop. And lie down. And move however I like whenever I want to."

The pisky abandoned the foil with a snort. "That's a pretty tall order for a girl in your position. You do realize I can do whatever I want with you now?"

"Can you let me go?" I asked hopefully.

"I could. But I'm not going to. I always appreciate a good jig. Don't you?"

Quicker than thought, my knees jerked to my chest in an animated burst of wild, ridiculous stepping. My arms curved over my head, fingers snapping. I leaped and danced about the small cell, unable to stop or even slow down.

"Okay! I get it!" I cried. "You're not going to give me a wish! You don't have to humiliate me too. I could have squashed you like a bug, but *I* was careful not to hurt *you.*"

My limbs jerked into a whole new, maniacal gear. The cell blurred as I jumped and whirled, completely out of control.

"Squashed me like a *what*?" the pisky asked dangerously.

"Like a . . . I mean a . . ." I knew firsthand how it felt to be compared to a bug—and when the creature in question had wings like a moth's, that was probably an extra-sensitive subject. "I just meant your wings are delicate. That's all I was trying to say."

"I have fine strong fliers," the pisky retorted. "Got me here and they'll see me gone too."

"I'm sorry!" I gasped, out of breath from the jig. "Just let me stop dancing before I drop dead!"

"That *has* happened," the pisky acknowledged. "Give me three magic words and I'll think about it."

Magic words? I was doomed.

"I don't know any magic!" I begged. "If these leprechauns had taught me anything useful, would I be stuck in here?"

My body lurched to a sudden stop.

"Nice point," the pisky admitted, moving toward the bars with its loot. I tried to reach for it, only to discover I was paralyzed again.

Then I realized the pisky was leaving.

"No! Stop! Don't leave me stuck here like a human statue!"

The creature stepped through the bars and cranked up its wings for takeoff. Its heavy load tipped its body forward as its heels lifted off the ledge.

"Please!" I cried.

The pisky hesitated, toes barely scraping stone. "I thought you didn't know any magic words."

"I don't! What magic words?" The answer hit me with a groan. "Please!" I shouted. "Pretty please! Pretty please with sugar on top!"

"There. Was that so hard?"

My feet released from the floor precisely as the pisky buzzed off into the moonlight. I threw myself against the bars, but the creature was already out of reach. I watched it fly across the clearing, juggling its awkward load.

Just at the edge of the pond, the button teetered off the pile. The pisky unclasped its hands to grab for it, and a Life Saver slipped from one skinny arm. Diving through the air, the pisky intercepted the button, but the candy fell to earth, landing in splashy wet mud. Its white edge reflected the moonlight as the pisky hovered indecisively above it.

My hand moved to my pocket. If the pisky liked peppermint so much, maybe I could still bargain with it. But before I could call out, the creature shrugged its scrawny shoulders and streaked off with the rest of its loot. I pushed my face up against the bars, straining to see where it had gone.

Then a new source of movement caught my eye.

Where the candy had fallen, something was rising out of the muck. Something weird and spindly and shaped like a . . . tree? Its pointed trunk stretched up toward the moon. Boughs sprouted and began to spread. The thing was growing at hyperspeed, as if someone had hit fast-forward on the movie of its life. Roots squelched down through mud, then twisted and writhed across dry dirt. Still the tree kept growing—up, out, bigger, faster, until it was truly huge. And every inch of root, trunk, and needle was peppermint white, glowing in the moonlight like a bleached bone.

I watched in awe as the roots reached wider, forcing boulders out of the ground, cracking them up against each other, pushing and grinding and knocking aside everything in their way.

What if I'd swallowed one of those Life Savers? I thought. The candy had looked completely normal until it got wet. *Good thing I don't like peppermint!*

But Gigi had. She'd loved it. Was it possible she'd never realized the danger she'd carried around in her sweater?

It never hurts to take a sweater. Her advice popped into my head as if waiting for that moment.

"She knew!" I gasped. "She *totally* knew!"

The candies were a magical insurance policy. Gigi had left them for me *knowing* I wouldn't eat them. I snatched the remaining ten out of my pocket and examined them in the moonlight: perfectly normal. If that pisky hadn't accidentally dropped one in water, I wouldn't have had a clue what they did.

That wasn't an accident, I realized. *It was luck!* Lexie's lucky charm had made the pisky drop that candy—and helped me hatch the plan forming in my mind now.

Setting a single Life Saver in the middle of my cell floor, I put the roll back in my pocket. Then I grabbed the bucket of water and slopped some over the candy.

Nothing happened for about five seconds. Then the candy began to melt, fusing to the stone. Hairlike white roots sprouted and spread. A tiny trunk unfurled and pointed toward the ceiling. Branches popped in all directions. The tree's top touched the ceiling and bent over sideways, still growing. Spreading, thickening limbs pushed me up against the cell wall. Grabbing the mattress, I huddled behind its padding and hoped I hadn't just made a big mistake.

The treetop found the window and pushed out between the bars. White branches writhed against the walls. And still the tree kept growing, its trunk thickening and straining. A massive crack rocked the cell as roots broke through the stone floor. Dry wood crunched, then exploded into splinters. Peering around my mattress, I saw a moonlit opening where the cell door used to be. But before I could figure out how to crawl through the branches to freedom, a rumbling shook the cell. The bent tree snapped upright as I ducked beneath my mattress, quivering under a sudden downpour of falling rocks.

When I finally dared to peek out again, I could barely

believe my eyes. The tree hadn't just destroyed the door; it had shattered the entire cell. Chunks of the hollowed boulder lay scattered all about. And towering above me, the tree stretched toward the full moon, still growing.

Shoving the mattress aside, I staggered to my feet. I was free! And, at least for the moment, there was no one around who knew that. What I did in the next few minutes could determine the rest of my life.

Leaping onto a branch of the peppermint tree, I took an elevator ride up its growing trunk, peering through the forest in an attempt to get my bearings. I couldn't locate the village, but far in the starry distance, a single dark pine poked above the horizon.

My tree stopped growing abruptly. I began scrambling down, half expecting to fall, but my flats gripped the chalky bark as if I'd turned into Spider-Man. Reaching the lowest branch, I jumped to the forest floor, landing easily.

I checked my sweater pocket. And then I took off running like I'd never run before.

Chapter 17

With such bright moonlight to guide me, I reached Kylie's keep in record time. I paused beneath the big pine long enough to make sure no one else was around. Then I rushed to the cave mouth.

But I didn't go inside.

The Scarlets' keep was in a ridge that stuck out from the mountain like a crooked foot, and that meant the cave had a natural exterior wall. Bypassing the entrance, I thrashed through the brush along the ridge's base, nervously trying to estimate how far down that wall I needed to go. I didn't have time to fool around, and I definitely didn't have time to make a mistake. When the Scarlets discovered that I'd escaped, I was pretty sure they wouldn't be throwing me another party.

A hundred feet back from the cave mouth, I took out three more Life Savers and balanced them on a ledge four feet up the wall. Then I started spitting. I was still wetting the third candy when the first one started sprouting. Dropping a final loogie, I backed away and took cover.

Three peppermint trees began growing so fast their trunks touched within a minute. Their roots burrowed deep into the ridge and intertwined on its surface, spreading and tangling, fighting for space. The narrow ledge beneath them exploded in a puff of dust, crushed by ravenous white roots and expanding trunks. Masses of branches collided, forcing the trees away from each other as they tilted up into the sky. Boulders cracked and groaned. The trio of magic trees forced every obstruction aside, setting off a chaos of tumbling rocks and uprooted bushes that made the ground tremble up through my shoes.

A little more, I thought. *Keep growing!*

The trees were nearly full height when a boom like a giant's cannon sent my hands over my ears. The ground lurched dizzily. I watched in awe as three enormous trees shuddered and dropped through the hollow ridge, crashing to earth in three different directions. Their toppling roots ripped the cave wall apart, hurling boulders into the air. Gravel pelted down like hail. And at the center of the destruction, a fresh hole gaped—my newly opened entrance into Kylie's inner keep.

I rushed toward the jagged opening, the warm light of an untold fortune in gold drawing me in like a vacuum. Scrambling upslope over rocks and roots, I slid down the rubble on the hole's other side into a tumbled golden sea of coins, nuggets, and bars.

Gold lust boiled through my blood again. I wanted to roll on a bed of nuggets, to stroke every gleaming bar, but there simply wasn't time. My ploy had bypassed the magic alarm, but someone was sure to have heard those falling trees and rocks. Running to the rear of the cave, I found the keeper's cot, grabbed two burlap bags with lashing cords, and sprinted back to where I'd come in.

Moonlight poured down on my head as I scooped up coins with both hands, one normal, one glowing like Rudolph's red nose. I had planned to fill each bag halfway, splitting up my load for easier carrying, but the bags got half full and I couldn't stop, loading in more handfuls until I could barely tie their tops closed. Then I stood up and tried to walk with a bag gripped in each hand.

I knew right away I had made a mistake—I couldn't even straighten my back. But no way was I leaving my new gold behind. Yanking the belt out of Gigi's sweater, I lashed one end to each bag and ducked my head through its middle, forming a yoke across my shoulders. Staggering under my load, I fought my way up to the exit hole and hesitated at its edge, praying I'd worked out all the magic. If I'd miscalculated somewhere, or there was yet another thing the leprechauns hadn't told me . . .

Drawing a deep breath, I stepped out with my gold. No invisible shield rose up to meet me. No leprechaun help required. I was free and clear!

Broken branches snagged my pants as I stumbled down through the fallen trees, but gold lust and adrenaline filled my veins, making me stronger than I'd ever dreamed. The bags actually seemed to get lighter as I walked on. Aiming for the heart of a pitch-dark thicket, I lost myself in its shadows just as the first Scarlet guards arrived, shouting with rage and disbelief at the sight of their broken keep.

I headed toward the village, keeping to the shadows and making quick progress. I was just beginning to hope I might be out of the search area when a posse of wild-eyed archers charged past a stone's throw away, arrows drawn and ready.

I froze behind a bush as they cut through a clearing, Lexie's warnings about shooting thieves ringing through my brain. There would be more archers about, ones who might do a better job of finding me. Forcing myself to move again, I dashed from tree to tree, daring to breathe only when my back was against the next trunk.

The sweater belt cut into my neck. My arms felt stretched to the breaking point. Common sense begged me to ditch the gold—or at least the extra bag—but I was way past listening to common sense. I was working under some completely different theory now, one in which gold was a living thing, something I'd no more abandon than a wounded best friend. I could feel its energy bubbling up through the bag tops, seeping into my blood, keeping me moving forward.

At last a few red lights came into view, glimmering through the trees. The excitement at the keep hadn't yet spread to the sleeping town. Remaining hidden in the woods, I worked my way along the town's outer edge until I could see the back of the Greens' guest cottage.

No lights were on in the hut, but outside in the yard, working alone by moonlight, Cain was harnessing the dog cart. All but two dogs were already hitched, and the corral gate stood open. I felt a rush of love for him and his crazy mustache. How had he guessed I'd be coming?

I nearly dashed out to meet him, but caution held me back. It was possible Scarlets were watching the cottage, and my situation would only get worse if I was caught with stolen gold. Untying the bags from my belt, I stuffed them deep beneath a bush. Then I retied my sweater, brushed myself off, and slunk into the yard.

Cain greeted me with a wry smile. "It was my watch with the dogs," he whispered. "I heard a bit o' thunder out by the keep, and my bones told me it'd be you. Did you get the gold?"

I was about to tell him everything when something in his

expression prickled the hairs on the back of my neck. Was I sure Cain could be trusted?

The last bit of advice from Gigi's letter screamed back into my brain: *Lying here is A-OK.*

I finally understood what she'd meant. She wasn't telling me to nap in the keep—she was telling me to *lie.* Just like all the leprechauns did. Like I'd been lied to by Kylie. Like Cain could be lying right now.

Lying here was more than okay; it was self-defense.

"I couldn't get any," I whispered back, saving the truth for Balthazar. "Let's just get the others and get out of here."

Cain's gaze turned suspicious.

He knows, I thought, panicking. *He's going to see the gold anyway. I'm wasting time!* I was just about to confess when Cain dropped his gaze.

"Go wake the others," he said. "I'll hitch this last pair."

He already had the dogs' harnesses on. I hurried across the yard, eager to wake Balthazar. I had just reached the cottage door when Cain cried out behind me. "Hie! Hie!"

Wheeling around, I saw him astride a lead dog, his hands gripping its ears and his heels dug in for all he was worth. The empty cart careened forward. I dashed after it as the dogs picked up speed, angling to cut them off at the gate. Launching myself like a football tackle, I sailed over the team and knocked Cain off his mount, trapping him under my body as we hit the ground.

The impact must have stunned him, or maybe he just couldn't breathe facedown in the dirt. Before he could muster a proper fight, I whipped off my trusty sweater belt and hogtied his hands to his feet. Flipping him onto his back, I read the truth in his lying eyes. Cain was the traitor I'd been looking for.

"Aw, Cain," I sighed. "I really liked you."

"I like you too, girl. What does that have to do with gold?"

Footsteps charged up behind me—Balthazar, red-faced and out of breath. I heard Fizz whistle for the dogs.

"We have to go *now*!" Balthazar barked. "Get in the cart, Lil. Leave this rogue to me."

Lights were beginning to fill nearby windows. Kneeling, Balthazar grabbed the ends of Cain's mustache, crisscrossed them through his mouth like a gag, and knotted them behind his head.

"Don't hurt him!" I begged as Balthazar pulled on Cain's whiskers with all his strength.

Ludlow stumbled out, half dressed and wearing a flannel nightcap. "Lilybet! What's hap—" he began.

"In the cart!" Balthazar shouted at him. "In the cart *now*!"

"Not dressed like this? My hat!"

"Leave it!" I said. Dashing back to my hiding place, I returned dragging the stolen gold.

Four sets of leprechaun eyes just about fell out of their heads. Fizz and Balthazar looked proud enough to burst, Cain looked furious, and I thought Ludlow might faint. Somehow he pulled himself together enough to help Balthazar hoist Cain into the wagon. I hefted the gold in with him and we all scrambled in beside it.

"Go, Fizz!" I cried as red lights spread from building to building. Shouts rang out over the town. There could be only seconds before Scarlet guards showed up. "Go, go, *go!*"

"Hie!" Fizz hollered. The dogs took off at rocket speed, knocking me over backward. I tumbled about with three leprechauns, two bags of gold, a random boot, some dog biscuits, and a bottle of clover ale before I was able to sit up again.

Fizz lay flattened to his dog, driving like a maniac. The cart bounced dangerously, threatening to throw us out with every bump. Ludlow held on with white knuckles, but Balthazar didn't seem concerned about our imminent death. His eyes went to the stolen gold and watered up like he wanted to cry.

"Did you, Lil?" he whispered, as if he barely dared to believe it. "Tell me true: did you *really*?"

"Aye, that I did," I replied, smiling broadly. "*Two* bags of Scarlet gold."

"And a lot of good if it gets us all killed," Ludlow whimpered.

"Silence, idiot!" Balthazar roared. "How dare you speak that way to the keeper o' the Clan o' Green?"

That was when it dawned on me. I was keeper. I was keeper *already*. And Ludlow had my key.

"Give it," I demanded, shoving my hand under his nose. "And if you tell me it's back with your hat, I'll throw you out of this wagon."

Ludlow went three shades paler, gripping the wagon rail for dear life.

"Fitting justice that would be," Balthazar said. "But the coward doesn't have your key. No, that's with the traitor here."

Leaning over the hogtied leprechaun, Balthazar felt unsuccessfully through the pouches on Cain's belt. Then he grabbed Cain's green lapels and yanked them in opposite directions, stripping the coat to Cain's waist. My gold chain was around Cain's neck; my key rested on his bare belly. But it was another sight that made me gasp. Just below Cain's right shoulder, a raised four-point scar disfigured his arm, swollen like an angry welt and glowing red in the moonlight.

I wasn't the only Green who'd been bitten by a pisky.

"By gold and by glory!" Balthazar exclaimed. "What is the meaning o' this?"

Before he could untie Cain's 'stache for the answer, Fizz cried out up front.

"Balthazar! Lil! They're coming!" Riding as if he were part of his dog, Fizz shouted his team into a turn. "Haw! Haw! *Hie!*"

The cart veered left so abruptly that I fell over again. Flat on my belly, I grabbed the railing and pulled my head up for a peek. We were flying across the front edge of town on an angle toward the bridge, and suddenly I realized how vulnerable we still were. If the Scarlets managed to cut us off before the river, we'd be trapped. I glanced backward over my shoulder. Surging after us like an angry red tide was an army of torch-wielding Scarlets.

"Fizz!" I yelled, terrified. "Hurry!"

And then I saw something even scarier. A gang of leprechauns riding fast dogs was charging toward us through the woods, followed by a tall, loping shadow that could only be Kylie. Ducking below the rail, I grabbed my keeper key and yanked it off over Cain's head. If I was going down, I wasn't going without that. Pulling the chain on around my neck, I peeked back up again.

We were nearly to the bridge. Its narrow arc rose over the river a hundred yards away. We were going to beat the mob on foot, but the pack riding dogs was closing fast.

"They're gaining," Balthazar said grimly.

"No, we'll make it," I said.

"Over the bridge, maybe, but that's not the border. We're all in a spot o' trouble now."

"All?"

"Aiding a gold thief," Ludlow moaned, "is punishable four different ways."

"You're completely safe, then," I retorted. "If we're caught, I'm going to tell everyone that you were no help at all!"

Even through his mustache gag, Cain snorted with laughter.

We raced through the tunnel of trees. Boards rumbled under our wheels as we hit the bridge. The Scarlets trailing on dogs were barely an arrow shot behind.

And suddenly I knew what I had to do.

Snatching the last six Life Savers out of my pocket, I started shredding off wax paper.

Balthazar's eyes bugged out. "Are those—?"

"Find me that bottle of ale. Hurry!"

He scrambled to trap it.

"Slow down, Fizz!" I shouted. "I'm getting out."

"Ho!" Fizz reined back the dogs. Stepping over Cain, I grabbed the ale from Balthazar and tumbled out the back of the moving cart.

"Go, go, go!" I shouted, scattering Life Savers on the narrow bridge as Fizz spurred his team on. The Scarlet dogs were nearly to the boards. Alone high above the river, I smashed the bottle's top against the bridge rail and sprayed fizzing ale on the candies.

I was not prepared for what happened next.

The Life Savers absorbed the ale instantly. For one horrifying split second, I thought I didn't have enough liquid. Then all six candies literally exploded into trees. Roots, branches, and trunks shot in all directions with a crack like heaven splitting. Wheeling around, I tried to run, but it was already too late. The dog cart reached the opposite bank as the bridge broke apart and I fell, plunging through the darkness beneath it.

I'm going to die, I thought, surprised by how calm I felt. There was nothing I could do to save myself now. My hand went to Gigi's key, one last good-bye.

I smacked into water so icy it took my breath away. Churning, swirling darkness closed over my head. My feet kicked instinctively. My arms flailed in the current. Every bit of calm deserted me as, lungs burning for breath, I tried to find my way up. My sweater snagged, then tangled in something submerged. Yanking and kicking and choking, I broke free all at once and popped up through the river's surface.

"Lilllll!" Balthazar's anguished cry hit my ears as I came up gasping for air.

"What?" I hollered back.

There was a split second of stunned silence. Then about a million leprechauns all started shouting at once.

"There she is! I see her!"

"This way, Lil! Over here!"

"Get her! Get her!"

"Keep your head down, Lil!"

I treaded a circle to get my bearings. On the Scarlets' side of the river, a whole town's worth of leprechauns swarmed up and down in frustration. The bridge was gone, having collapsed just in time to strand the Scarlets on dogs with the others. And in the middle of the river, stopping me from drifting downstream with the current, a tangle of fallen peppermint trees choked my chunk of water like some sort of trippy beaver dam.

I grabbed a white branch. The once-chalky bark felt slick in my hand. *It's dissolving,* I realized. *Like* normal *Life Savers do.*

I suddenly wondered if other candies made magic here too—and if so, what they did—but I didn't have time to think about that. Balthazar was standing in the cart atop the other bank, jumping up and down and waving his hat frantically.

"Lil! Pull yourself across on the trees, Lil!"

But I didn't need help from the trees. Glancing back, I smiled to see that not a single Scarlet had ventured down to the water after me. *Leprechauns don't swim.* So long as no one shot me, I had it made.

Pushing off the dissolving tree, I kicked toward Balthazar.

In water safety class, they'd taught us to ditch loose clothes and shoes during emergency swims, but I wasn't about to part with Gigi's sweater or the silver flats. They churned like miniature swim fins, propelling me along.

"Look at our Lil!" Balthazar bragged. "She's *swimming*!"

I angled up current, swimming strong and enjoying myself despite the freezing water. Not only had I escaped the Scarlets, but the Greens were cheering me on like an Olympian. Fizz stood upright on his dog, Ludlow jumped wildly next to Balthazar, and even Cain had wriggled his head up over the rail. I did a few backstrokes, showing off. When I flipped over again, the Greens were hollering their heads off.

"It's not *that* hard," I called modestly, lifting a hand to wave. That was when I realized my team was no longer cheering. They were pointing behind me.

Kylie was at the river's edge, kicking off his boots. As I watched, he stripped off his vest and shirt and splashed into the water, egged on by the screaming crowd above.

Leprechauns don't swim. But Kylie did.

Putting my face in the water, I started kicking for all I was worth. As soon as I cleared the fallen trees, the current became stronger, fighting me for every inch. I could practically feel Kylie gaining on me, making me afraid to lose even the second it would take to glance back. At last my fingertips raked slimy gravel. Gathering my legs beneath me, I found my footing and charged up out of the shallows.

"Run, Lilybet! Hurry!" Ludlow cried anxiously.

The slope between me and the cart was steep and slippery. Loose rocks spurted from beneath my shoes. Grabbing protruding roots, I pulled myself up over the bank's edge and belly flopped in the dirt at its top. Rolling to a crouch, I turned and braced for impact with Kylie.

To my amazement, he was dog-paddling back to the opposite shore, his own clan booing and jeering as he returned in soggy disgrace.

Fizz drove up alongside me. "Never made it halfway out," he reported. "Not a bit o' the swimmer you are, Lil."

"Aye, true enough," Balthazar said. "But there could still be sentries this side o' the water, so if you two don't mind gloating later . . ."

I jumped into the wagon, sprawling on top of my stolen gold. "Go, Fizz! Go!" I cried. If I had learned anything, it was to listen to Balthazar.

I took one last look at Kylie's miserable silhouette as he hauled himself out of the river. Then the cart found the road, and we were off, riding full speed for the border.

Balthazar, Ludlow, and I watched tensely in all directions, holding our breath against a surprise attack from behind the rocks and trees crowding our winding path. Finally, the trees started to thin. We passed the last patch of rocks.

Nothing but clover spread out before us.

"Is this . . . Are we over the border?" I asked hopefully.

"Not yet." Balthazar stared straight ahead as if we might still be ambushed from beneath a clump of clover.

"When?"

"You'll know."

I had no idea how I was supposed to know, in the dark, when the border wasn't even marked. I'd only been over it once, and I'd been a little preoccupied at the time. *If the sun were out, I'd be able to tell by the clover,* I thought. *Maroon on their side, green on ours.*

I squinted up at the moon, trying to gauge how much longer until daylight. Then I looked back down and gasped.

"My hands!" I cried, holding them up. Even by moonlight I could tell my right one was no longer red. They both looked completely normal.

Balthazar took one glance at me and smiled as if his birthday and Christmas had come on the same day. "Didn't I tell you you'd know? That's the amnesty, Lil!"

"You mean . . . ?"

"Aye, free and clear, every one o' us. Might as well o' never happened." His grin stretched impossibly wider. "Except for this," he added, thumping the nearest sack of gold.

Chapter 18

The sun was high and warm when we rolled back into the Meadows. The dogs pranced as they pulled our cart through town. Balthazar held a bag of stolen gold up over his head, and crowds of Greens ran out to meet us, cheering until they were hoarse. I sat tall in the wagon, my keeper key gleaming around my neck, and basked in their admiration.

I deserve this, I thought happily. *I totally kicked Scarlet butt!*

Mother Sosanna and her council were waiting on the dais in Green Field. I walked boldly into their presence accompanied by raucous cheers. Guards prodded a bare-chested Cain up the stairs behind me, his wrists shackled and his wet mustache still tied through his mouth. His puffy pisky scar oozed nastiness in the sunshine, so inflamed as to be almost unrecognizable.

Hustling up between us, Balthazar bowed to the council. "Lilybet Green has passed her final test," he said. "She awaits your confirmation. Meanwhile, this weasel"—he kicked Cain behind one knee—"is a traitor to his clan. He tried to make Lilybet fail!"

Gasps ripped through the crowd. Sosanna looked alarmed.

"Why would he do that?" she asked me.

"I don't know, but he tried to run off with the dogs and get me caught with stolen gold. Maybe it's to do with that cold-succession thing, but if Cain and I are in the same line, I don't see how that works. Do you?"

Mother Sosanna looked absolutely stunned.

"It could be anything!" Balthazar put in nervously. "Look at him—he's pisky bit!"

The leprechauns packing the field babbled with shock and excitement, straining forward to see.

"Ungag the prisoner," Sosanna demanded.

A blade flashed in a guard's hand and Cain's knotted mustache fell to the ground, cut loose from his lip on both sides. A caterpillar's length of trembling whiskers was all that remained, making him look somehow smaller.

"Cain Green!" Sosanna said. "I will know your involvement in this. Explain immediately."

"He'll lie!" I whispered to Balthazar.

"Not to the chief, Lil. Pain o' death—and she'll know, believe me."

Cain shot Balthazar a nasty look, then bowed before the council. "Not much to tell, is there?" he rasped. "Had the key, got an itch, and caught myself a pisky."

"I'll have details!" Sosanna insisted.

Cain heaved an enormous sigh. "When our Maureen passed on and the key flashed its beacon home, I found it first, didn't I? I reclaimed eight bags o' Maureen's gold for the clan, and I won the honor o' guarding the key for our next keeper. I was the one who held it safe—until you chose *him* and his lads for delivery," Cain said with a disgusted nod toward Balthazar.

"Yes, yes," Sosanna said impatiently. "Everyone already knows that."

Not everyone, I thought, fascinated. Eight "reclaimed" bags of gold could explain a lot about where Gigi's money had disappeared to!

"So I had the key, didn't I?" Cain went on. "The key to the whole inner keep in a wee pouch on my belt. But I couldn't use it."

"O' course you couldn't," Balthazar broke in. "You're a leprechaun!"

"Shh!" Sosanna hushed him.

Cain gave Balthazar a superior look. "Right," he said at last. "A *leprechaun* can't use the key. But a leprechaun with one bitty drop o' human blood could."

Horrified gasps ran through the crowd.

"No such creature exists!" Mother Sosanna objected. "That would be . . . that would be a reverse lepling! How could such a thing even be possible?"

"The pisky bite," I said.

Cain grinned ruefully. "Aye," he admitted, "a scheming horror o' a pisky, wasn't it? Gave me a good nip too. But I caught it fair and square, and it had to give me a wish."

Balthazar looked ready to hurl. "You asked to have *human* blood in your veins?"

"Hey!" I protested. "Don't say that like it's an insult."

"Beg pardon, Lil, but—" Balthazar shuddered convulsively, along with the council and most of the crowd. "No sane leprechaun would dream o' doing that."

"Aye, and where's the leprechaun who could stay sane with that key in his hands?" Cain asked. "It called me out o' sleep! Tormented me every second o' seven days and nights. 'Keep me. Use me,' it begged. 'All the riches o' the clan will be yours.'"

"Can the key really talk?" I asked Balthazar.

"No!" he scoffed.

"It talked to *me*!" Cain insisted. "I heard it, didn't I? Over and over . . . the gold!" He moaned. "All that gold."

The lust in his eyes was a fever, a sickness he couldn't control. Remembering my time in both keeps, I almost understood. I had felt that fever myself—and I was only the teensiest part leprechaun.

"So, you caught a pisky," I filled in for him. "And what did you ask it for?"

"Your exact words!" Sosanna admonished.

Cain sighed again, remembering. "I held that pisky tight and said, 'I wish I had the teeniest wee drop o' human blood in me veins, just enough to use the key.'"

The crowd recoiled in revulsion. Sosanna looked equally repulsed, but she sensed there must be more.

"Is that all?" she prodded.

"'Just enough to use the key'," Cain repeated unhappily, "'while the council makes the coming keeper tests so hard that Lil will fail one o' them, and every candidate behind her will fail too.' Without a new keeper, I could have gone on using the key for as long as it took me to steal all the gold."

Outraged shouts filled the field. The ladies of the council looked faint. Sosanna turned deathly pale as a sort of film evaporated off her eyes, a shadow of something so slight I couldn't see it until it had gone.

"Bepiskied!" she gasped. "Me! And my entire council?"

The furious crowd surged forward. In a flash, Cain's guards became his protectors, preventing a wave of angry leprechauns from mobbing the platform.

"Enough!" Sosanna roared.

Everyone froze in place. The shouts died into mutters.

"Can I ask a question?" I ventured. "Cain, wouldn't it have been easier to just ask the pisky to give you the gold?"

"Aye," he said, "but the magic protecting that gold is a leprechaun's, isn't it? No pisky can undo an existing spell, especially not one o' our spells on gold."

"True. Very true," Balthazar agreed, looking relieved.

"But with the key and the blood, I could help myself. At least I should o' been able to." Cain spat on his boots. "Piskies!"

I tried to figure out what had gone wrong with his wish. Which part had the pisky twisted? "Did you get the human blood?" I asked. "How did the pisky do that?"

"Why, took it from you, o' course."

"Me?" It was my turn to be flabbergasted.

"Did I know it would be that way, Lil? I never asked for *your* blood."

"Be what way?" I asked suspiciously.

For the first time since he'd been caught, Cain hung his head. "The knife, the kitchen, that mark on your hand . . ."

Flipping my left hand over, I stared at the scar on my palm. My accident after Gigi's memorial service hadn't been an accident at all? "I never saw a pisky," I said skeptically.

"Well you wouldn't, in Providence. Just took a quick sip, then back to me." Cain nodded down at his oozing scar. "Punched it right in there."

Balthazar turned a bilious shade of green. I felt a little sick myself.

"So let me get this straight. You're a lepling now?"

Cain grimaced. "I wouldn't say *that*."

"Your blood is mixed, like mine," I insisted. "Your blood is mixed *with* mine."

"Just the teeniest bit. One bitty drop."

"That *drop* took eight stitches. I'm glad you didn't ask for a pint!"

"I didn't wish for you to cut yourself, did I? Maybe that was going to happen anyway."

"Right," I said skeptically.

"Piskies take advantage!" he maintained.

I looked to Balthazar and the council. They nodded grudgingly, conceding the possibility.

Sighing, I moved on. "I'd like to know how you took gold out of the inner keep without passing three keeper tests. And how did you carry it from the outer keep if you're not a full leprechaun anymore?"

Cain shook his head with obvious disgust.

"You couldn't!" I exclaimed. "*That's* how the pisky got you!"

"It didn't get me! Lying cheat o' a pisky! You were supposed to fail your tests, weren't you? And I was digging a tunnel out—all I needed was time. But that pisky went back on my wish, that's what, and that's against the rules!"

Despite their grievances against him, the council looked disturbed. "Piskies twist, but they don't lie," one of the ladies said. "Are you certain of your wish, Cain?"

"O' course I'm certain!" he shouted. "Would I foul up something so important? I wished for Lil and all the others to fail one o' their keeper tests."

The council conferred worriedly, but I felt myself starting to smile. "You said *tests*. I should fail a *test*."

"Aye," Cain agreed.

"And I did. I messed up that gold theft big-time. And then I tried again. I *did* fail a test, Cain, but I passed my trial."

His bushy brows twisted as he followed that one. Then his face went slack. "O' all the . . . Filthy piskies!"

"So all this time," I asked him, "when you were pretending to help me, you were really just there to make certain I failed?" A barely remembered scrap of conversation came back to me. "*You* convinced Maxwell to pack my key in fireworks! You said it would add flash!"

Cain's head dropped even lower. "Helped him too—then

added a dash more when Maxie wasn't looking. Just enough to scare you off, Lil! Had to protect my investment, didn't I?"

"Cain Green," said Sosanna, "I've heard enough! You have broken the ban on pisky wishing, you have bepiskied me and the entire council, you have attempted to steal clan gold, and you have caused harm and aggravation to your sister Lilybet."

Harm and aggravation? I thought with a smile. *Wait until she hears what happened in the Hollow!*

"You are sentenced to exile in the Wastes," Sosanna decreed. "For life."

Cain slumped as if he'd been shot. Two of his guards caught him before he hit the floor. The council stared him down unmercifully, but in the crowd around the platform, I spotted pitying faces. The Wastes was obviously not a nice place.

The guards started marching Cain off the platform. "Stand on your feet, maggot!" one of them snapped as Cain's legs buckled.

"Wait!" I cried.

Everyone turned to me in surprise. I was surprised myself. But when Cain's eyes met mine, I knew what I had to do. He was my brother, my *blood* brother, and despite everything, I kind of liked him.

"Is there anyone here who hasn't felt the pull of gold?" I

asked, addressing the whole crowd. "The way it gets into your blood and pumps through your veins like a fever?"

I could tell by their faces they knew that fever well.

"That's part of being a leprechaun, isn't it?" I asked. "I've felt it myself. In the keep, surrounded by all those coins and nuggets, the bars stacked up to the ceiling . . . That gold shines with its own light. It hums like a lullaby and beats like a heart. Gold comes alive for us. Am I right?"

"Aye. Aye." The field was a sea of nodding heads.

"And I have hardly any leprechaun blood, so if *I* feel that way, I can only imagine what a temptation holding that key was to Cain. Can *you* imagine?" I asked them. "Would every one of you have been strong enough to resist?"

Hundreds of gazes dropped to the clover.

"What Cain did was wrong," I continued, "and I suppose he has to be punished. But he was *sick*. Doesn't he deserve a little mercy too?"

No one answered. Nobody looked at me either, no one except Cain. His eyes flowed over with gratitude until fat tears dripped to the ground.

"Lilybet, you speak with insight beyond your years," Sosanna said at last. "We are humbled by your forgiveness. You may decide Cain's punishment."

"*Me?*" That was pretty much the last thing I'd expected. Or wanted. Everyone was looking at me, though. And I'd opened my mouth, so . . .

"Cain Green," I began. "Stand up, okay?"

The guards placed Cain over his boots again, and somehow he stayed there, tottering uncertainly.

"Cain Green, for bepiskying the council and trying to steal the clan's gold, I sentence you to . . ." I thought desperately. ". . . community service! Someone has to pick up after all these dogs, right? That's you, Cain, for the next two years."

Appreciative snickers ran through the crowd.

"Also, you can't grow a mustache for five years, since that's how long you nearly got me imprisoned for."

Cain's expression said he found that especially harsh, but I wasn't done yet. "And you will use your own personal gold to pay back what I stole plus damages in the Hollow. Let's see, that's a wooden bridge, a stone jail cell, a thoroughly busted-up keep, and probably a few other things I'm forgetting right now."

Cain staggered but stayed on his feet. The other Greens cheered wildly.

"Lastly," I shouted over the noise, "you owe me three favors, Cain, to be collected whenever I say." I had no idea what I'd ask him for, but if I was going to be hanging around the Meadows, favors were sure to come in handy. "Okay. I'm done."

Sosanna nodded. "Very wise, Lilybet. Let it be."

Another huge cheer went up. The next second I was

mobbed by leprechauns. They swarmed onto the platform, surrounding my legs, reaching their hands up to me, jostling and pushing and crowding until I could barely stay on my feet.

"Lil-y-bet! Lil-y-bet! Lil-y-bet! *Greeeeeeeeen!*"

"You guys!" I protested, stumbling. "You're going to knock me down!"

"Fall back, Lil!" Balthazar urged. "We've got you!"

I resisted another second, and then I let go, tumbling backward onto the eager hands of dozens of cheering Greens. It felt like my body went weightless, floating on the gentle support of a living magic carpet. Hands moved underneath me, passing me from Green to Green. Across the platform, down the stairs, out over the grass . . .

"Lil-y-bet! Lil-y-bet! Lil-y-bet! *Greeeeeeeeen!*"

And beneath a perfect aqua sky, thousands of cheering leprechauns crowd-surfed me around that field like a rock star.

Chapter 19

"Lilybet Green, you are our keeper," Sosanna said, leaning out on her stool to kiss my cheek. "May your work bring you joy."

"Thank you." I turned back to the crowd in Green Field, but for once they weren't all cheering. Instead, thousands of brimming eyes gazed up at me, touched by the solemn moment. I was pretty touched myself, but I'd already done enough crying to last a lifetime.

"Aw, come on, you guys," I said. *"Greeeeeeeeen!"* The call flew out of my throat as if it had been stuck there for years, just waiting for that moment. The sound boomeranged over the field and came back multiplied.

"*Greeeeeeeeen!*" my clan shouted in unison. "Lilybet! Lilybet! *Greeeeeeeeen!*"

And then the cheering began again, along with a bright green blizzard of slingshot-fired confetti. I jumped off the edge of the platform and ran through the field to the cottage, eager to pack my things for home.

I was already at the tall cupboard, throwing Gigi's clothes onto the bed, when the first leprechauns reached my open front door. Balthazar, at the front of the pack, did his best to block the doorway. "Lil! Lil!" he puffed, crimson-faced. "You have a few transfers out here."

"Transfers?" I crossed the room to find a hundred leprechauns in my front yard, some holding heavy bags, others empty sacks. With a sinking feeling, I realized what they wanted.

They wanted me to do my *job.*

"Now?" I said. "This minute?"

"Folk have been waiting a long time, Lil," Balthazar reminded me, but there was new respect in his tone. The gazes of the others were pleading. I suddenly understood what it truly meant to be keeper: They weren't telling me anymore. They were *asking* me. I had every right to say no and rush home to my mother—my deeply worried, soon-to-be-furious mother.

"I suppose I could do a few transfers," I said, inspiring happy shouts. "But only a few! You've waited this long; you can wait a few more days while I straighten things out at home."

"Very wise, Lilybet," Balthazar said, bowing.

"I *am* very wise, but you've got to drop the act," I teased. "I don't know who you are when you're not driving me crazy. Hey, Lexie!" I cried, spotting her at the back of the crowd. "Lexie, hi! Let her come up, you guys."

The mob parted grudgingly, casting envious looks at Lexie as she hurried to my door.

"Lil, you did it!" she said. "Congratulations!"

"Thanks, but I wouldn't be here without your help. Your lucky charm saved the day."

"Really?" Lexie looked thrilled.

"I'd actually started thinking that button wasn't lucky at all. Then, right when I least expected it, it totally came through."

"That's how luck is," she told me, grinning. "Luck never shows up when you're looking; it happens on its own terms. So where's the button, then? Why aren't you wearing it?"

My face fell. "I'm sorry, Lexie. A pisky took it."

"But . . . *Another* pisky?"

Oohs and aahs from the crowd reminded me they were still listening. "Everyone, go wait by the keep," I directed. "I'll be there in a minute."

Leprechauns stampeded my doorway, Balthazar barely managing to hold them back. "Go *around,* you idiots! Does Lilybet want the entire clan tramping through her hut?"

My hut, I thought, smiling, as they diverted off around the cottage. It felt strange and a little awesome to have a place of my own. Not that I wasn't still anxious to get back to Providence.

"So, I'll do some quick transfers, then what?" I asked. "How soon can we leave?"

"One last bit o' business and you're on your way," Balthazar promised.

I'd been around the Greens long enough to spot a leprechaun snow job. "What sort of business?" I asked suspiciously.

"Practically nothing!" he assured me, wide-eyed. "Just the standard clover swear that you will never reveal the folk's existence or divulge anything about us to anyone until such time as your successor is ready for her trial, at which time you'll speak only to her."

"Oh." That didn't sound so bad. Except . . . "What am I supposed to tell my mom?"

Balthazar shrugged. "Would she believe you anyway, Lil?"

He had me there. I was pretty much dead either way. In fact, I could actually see things going worse if I started ranting on about my time with the little people.

"Fine. I'll take the swear. But you guys owe me

something too. What about the luck I was supposed to get when I became keeper? What about my allowance?"

"You already got the luck, Lil," Lexie said, touching a finger to her cheek. "You've been kissed by Mother Sosanna!"

I made a face, disappointed. I'd been hoping for a lucky gold ring or talisman—something with a lot more flash than a kiss. Unless maybe it had left a mark . . .

Running over to the tub, I rummaged through the toiletries there until I found a small mirror. My cheek looked exactly the same.

"What are you looking for, silly?" Lexie asked, giggling. "You can't see luck! You wear it like you wear your skin. Luck is part o' you now, Lil. No one can ever take it away."

"Really?" If that were true, then maybe Sosanna's kiss was better than a ring—although still sadly lacking in flash. "How about my allowance?"

Balthazar stepped forward, looking shifty again. "I have an accounting o' that right here," he said, pulling a scrap of paper from his coat.

"Dog cart travel for both trips, one thousand nine hundred thirty-five dymers," he read aloud. "Feasting, thirty-four deloreans. Fireworks and leprechaun lights, nine hundred thirty-two class-A nuggets. Four-man escort from Providence—"

"Yeah, I know this one. Priceless," I said.

"No. Twelve deloreans," he corrected seriously.

"Are you reading me a *bill*?" I asked, incredulous.

"Not a bill, Lil. Expenses. It's traditional for the keeper to bear the cost o' her initiation."

"Is it traditional for the keeper to get her butt thrown in jail and nearly drown falling through a bridge?" I shouted, outraged. "Is it traditional for her to get assigned a couple of suicide missions by a bepiskied council?"

"Now, Lil. You did destroy that bridge yourself, so you really can't hold the clan—"

"I'm not paying for that stuff! You guys owe *me,* and you owe me big!"

I looked to Lexie for backup.

"Sorry, Lil," she said miserably. "It's in the bylaws. The new keeper always pays."

"You've got to be . . . Fine," I gave in, just wanting to get home. "How much is a delorean? Wait, never mind. Just tell me how much I'm getting after you subtract all that stuff."

Balthazar smiled with relief. "Not to worry, Lil. You'll have this all worked off in a couple o' years."

"A couple of years!"

"We didn't charge you for the keeper key," he offered.

"The key isn't actually mine, is it?"

"True enough," he admitted. "It belongs to the clan. Although some folk think we could charge you rent."

"Rent?" I had to take a couple of breaths before I could speak without shrieking. "This is completely unfair."

"Nobody likes it at first," he admitted. "But you're only thirteen yet, and you'll earn plenty o' gold, Lil. More than you'll ever need."

Maybe so, I thought, but I'd already learned this much about gold: the desire to possess it wasn't about need.

"Right, then!" he said brightly. "We'll just pop over to the keep and make those transfers, shall we?"

I followed him out my back door, still fuming about the deductions from my allowance. But the sun was shining brightly in the field behind the cottage, and the crowd waiting at the keep cheered the moment I stepped outside. Lexie skipped along beside me, her pride at being my friend obvious. *And she* is *my friend,* I realized with wonder. *I really care about her.*

I cared about Balthazar too. And Bronny and Kate and Sosanna and Fizz, and even Cain. They weren't the friends I'd been hoping for, but there was a bond between us now, one I felt certain would last all my life. "Good things *do* come in small packages," I said, laughing.

"And monstrously large ones," Lexie said, smiling back.

The first thing I noticed in the outer keep were the two bags of gold I had stolen, waiting to be counted and stored. I opened the magic wall, dragged them over the threshold to safety, and walked back to the desk. Opening the ancient ledger to a new page, I dipped an old-fashioned pen into green ink and broke out my best handwriting:

Here begins the Accounting of Lilybet Green
in the first year of her service as
Keeper of the Clan of Green.

"How come this ink doesn't bleed through the paper?" I asked Lexie.

"Magic," she replied. "Enchanted gold dust all through it. Holds a memory spell too. Anything you read or write in enchanted ink will come back to you when you need it most."

Gigi's clues, for example, I realized, smiling. "I wish they used this stuff at school. I'd never have to study for tests again!"

The next two hours were busy. Balthazar escorted leprechauns in one at a time, and while deposits meant only a line of writing plus a count to make sure the gold was all there, each withdrawal had to be tracked down, bagged, and carried by me personally to the outer keep.

Lexie was a huge help, teaching me the leprechaun coins, and how to class the nuggets, and how many dymers were in a delorean, and tons of other useful stuff. Balthazar kept order until the line finally cleared out.

At last I was free to go home.

I was about to close the magic wall when Mother Sosanna and her council walked into the outer keep. "Have you forgotten to add that gold to the count, Lilybet?" Sosanna asked, pointing to my stolen bags.

"Oh. Yeah. I'll catch it next time."

"Balthazar?" she prompted. "The clover swear?"

Scurrying outside, he uprooted a hunk of clover and ran back in to us. I crushed a few leaves into goop while Sosanna did the same.

"You will never reveal the folk's existence or anything about us to anyone but your successor, and only then when it's her turn to try," Sosanna said.

"I swear," I said, swapping juicy wrists.

She smiled happily. "Well, then, Lilybet. I understand you would like to return to Providence now?"

"Yes. Please."

"And you will come back regularly?"

"I'll come back, but we have to work out a better schedule, because I can't be spending two days in a dog cart every time you guys need to do some banking. I have a life, you know, not to mention a mother who asks lots of questions." I felt kind of queasy even thinking about those questions—and all the answers I wouldn't have.

"You needn't worry so much about time," Sosanna said with a gentle smile. "Time passes faster as you age, Lilybet, and the Meadows is very old indeed. Nevertheless, now that you're our keeper, there's a swifter way to travel."

"I'm all about swift," I said.

"Simply open a door," she told me. "Take your keeper key

in hand, picture where you want to go, open any door, and step through it. You're there."

I gasped. "Really?"

"We can't have you riding two days in a dog cart every time we need you," she said, eyes twinkling.

"So, like . . . I could go home right now? This minute?"

"Come and go as you wish, Lilybet."

No wonder Caspar was whining about doors back in Providence! And no wonder Balthazar didn't want me to see one—I'd have been gone before they could blink!

I was about to raise the security wall once again when my eyes landed on the two bags of Scarlet gold still lashed closed with crimson cords. The first inklings of a new idea stirred inside my brain.

I stepped back into the inner keep. "You know what? I will count this gold before I leave."

Untying the heavier bag, I took out a handful of coins and held them into the light.

"Condors, those are!" someone cried. "Scarlet gold for sure!"

"Does Scarlet gold look . . . scarlet?" I asked Balthazar. "These coins seem kind of rosy."

"Never heard o' that," Balthazar answered, edging up beside me. "Different denominations, to be sure, but not color."

"It's pink," I insisted. "You don't see that?"

He put his whole head into the bag, happy for any excuse to get closer. "Looks gold," he grunted at last.

"I don't think so." Glancing over my shoulder, I spotted Ludlow in the crowd. "Ludlow! Come help me!"

He skittered up, blushing with pleasure to have been singled out. "At your service, Lilybet!"

I pulled the bag over the threshold. "Carry this gold outside for me, will you? I want to see it in the sunshine."

"My pleasure, Lilybet!"

Balthazar looked as if I'd just punched him in the gut. *He'll thank me later,* I thought, locking the security wall and following Ludlow.

Ludlow dragged the bag through the outer keep, his leprechaun strength almost outmatched by the combination of so much gold and his small stature. I heard Balthazar grumbling that he could have done it faster—and without sweating too—as Ludlow finally pulled the sack through the cave mouth and onto the clover outside. "Is this . . . far enough?" he panted.

"A little farther," I said, squinting up at the sun, then across the field at the keeper's cottage. Ninety-eight percent of the crowd was still in the cave behind us. Only a few scattered leprechauns dotted the open field. One of them was Cain, freshly shaved. He shuffled along listlessly, both eyes on the ground and a poop scooper clutched in his hands.

Ludlow dragged the bag five more feet.

"Perfect!" I said, snatching it from him and making a run for the hut.

"Lil!" Balthazar cried, horrified.

A few shocked leprechauns tried to muster a chase as I sprinted over the clover. I had a head start, though, not to mention longer legs. My silver flats ate up the field. I blew past a startled Cain before he had time to react. Glancing back, I saw one of Balthazar's guards gaining fast.

"Cain! Favor one!" I cried.

Cain's boot flashed out, catching the running guard's legs and sending him sprawling. A spark returned to Cain's green eyes as he smiled with satisfaction.

Grabbing the key around my neck, I pictured my bedroom in Providence and lunged for the hut's back door. The knob turned. My foot touched the threshold. The doorframe filled with a swirling blur of neither here nor there.

"Ha! Amnesty! I have amnesty!" I cried. Pausing on the border the opened door had created, I turned to the crowd catching up behind me. "And serves you right too! You want expenses? Fine. I want this *extra* bag I stole from the Scarlets."

I was prepared for just about anything. Some sort of major tantrum seemed likely. My clan stared in stunned disbelief.

And then they started laughing.

"Oh, she's a shrewd one!" Balthazar cried, delighted. "I told you our Lil was a keeper!"

"Crafty, that was!" a chorus of voices agreed.

"Slyful like I've never seen!"

Ludlow stumbled up, completely out of breath. "Lilybet!" he whined. "You tricked me!"

"Aye." I caught Cain's eye and winked. "What does that have to do with gold?"

The leprechauns laughed and laughed as Mother Sosanna made her way forward. "Cleverly done, Lilybet," she said. "You may keep your prize."

"And you can't punish Cain for helping," I said. "The entire clan agreed he had to give me three favors."

"True enough," she acknowledged. "His assistance must be overlooked."

Dipping into the open bag, I flipped a condor to Lexie. "For luck!" I called. "See you soon!"

Gold flashed like solid sunshine as the coin tumbled through the air and landed in Lexie's small hands. "Soon!" she called back merrily, brandishing her new lucky charm.

With a last wave to my laughing clan, I stepped through the cottage door and closed it firmly behind me.

Chapter 20

Everything went dark. All I saw was black. I experienced an instant of pure panic.

And then I felt the doorknob still clutched in my hand. Twisting it hurriedly, I pushed the door open again.

Light replaced the darkness. I was standing in the doorway of my own bedroom, looking into a familiar hall.

Home!

I nearly shouted for joy. Then I remembered what I was wearing. And the gold still in my hands. Explaining my absence would be hard enough without adding in Gigi's sweater and a bag full of leprechaun coins. Easing the door shut, I retreated into my bedroom and did a silent happy dance. Then I stashed the gold beneath my bed and grabbed some clean clothes to change into.

I barely recognized the girl who stared back from the bathroom mirror. My hair looked different, of course. And, honestly, I could have used a bath. But beneath those spikes and smudges was a pair of too-wide eyes brimming with new confidence. My complexion glowed in a way that would make any girl feel lucky. I looked ready to take on the world.

I could only hope I was ready to take on my mother.

Stripping off Gigi's sweater and shirt, I stepped out of her jeans without taking off my flats. The leotard and shorts I'd worn a week before still lay on the floor where they'd dropped. Kicking them aside, I pulled on a green T-shirt and white shorts. Then, with Gigi's clothes wadded under one arm, I headed for my closet to change shoes. Halfway across the room, the silver flats on my feet morphed into green-and-white sneakers.

I stopped and stared in disbelief. The shoes had transformed before my eyes.

They're magic! I realized, awed. *But how? Leprechauns can only enchant gold, and these shoes are made of silver.*

The obvious truth finally hit me. *Not silver. White gold.*

The shoes' cobbler had the touch! No wonder Horace Green shoes were such a big deal. On top of everything else they did, they coordinated with outfits! I smiled, imagining the possibilities as I stashed Gigi's clothes and pulled on a sweatshirt to cover my keeper key.

Opening my bedroom door, I ran into the hall. "Mom!" I called at the top of my lungs. "I'm home!"

"Lily? Lily!" She came running out of the den so fast we nearly collided in the kitchen. "Thank God!"

I caught only a glimpse of her worried, tear-streaked face before she wrapped me in a hug and started squeezing the life out of me. "Where have you been? I've been so worried!"

I hugged her back almost as hard. "I'm really sorry, Mom. I never meant to worry you, or leave the house, or anything bad."

"Okay. It's okay," she said, crying into my hair. Then she pushed me out to arm's length and took a long, anxious look. "Are you all right?"

"Yes, fine. Just sorry, like I said."

Mom took a deep breath. "Has anybody hurt you?"

"No, nothing like that. Nothing bad happened to me." Nothing I could tell her about, anyway, thanks to Sosanna's clover swear.

"Let me see your head." She started searching through my pixie, parting my hair every which way. My heart sank as I realized she was looking for blast injuries. That "bitty pop o' sparks" on our porch was going to be darn hard to explain.

"I'm not hurt, Mom. I promise."

She checked my whole head anyway, then took another, relieved, breath. "Well, it's definitely not as bad as I feared. Candy Douglas made it sound like you were singed down to your scalp!"

"Really?" I said weakly. "Hmm."

"I need to sit." Mom dropped into a chair at the kitchen table, her eyes still roaming over every inch of me. I sat across from her.

"Who cut your hair?" she asked at last.

"Um . . ." Would I even be allowed to say Kate's name? "Just some girl I met."

"Met where, Lily? Where have you been all night?"

"Well, uh . . . Wait. All *night*?"

Hallelujah! I thought. So Sosanna had been telling the truth about time.

"Don't act like you don't know how long it's been!" Mom scolded. "And how did you get back into the house?"

"Um, through my bedroom?"

"I thought I locked that window! This house . . . I don't know, Lily. Maybe we should move."

"Not again!" I begged.

She looked surprised. "I thought you hated it here."

"I do. I mean . . . I did. I'm getting used to it, I guess. At least I'm friends with Kendall now." *If she's still speaking to me,* I added silently. "I just don't want to move again. Please."

"Well, the neighbors are nice." Mom sighed. "Although if I were you, I wouldn't expect to babysit again anytime soon."

"No," I said glumly.

"Where did you go, Lily? I looked everywhere."

"Just to the park. And then, you know . . . around." Inspiration struck. "I couldn't say, exactly."

"You weren't at one of your friend's houses? You didn't ride in someone's car?"

"No. I promise."

"Who is this girl you were hanging out with?"

"What? Oh, her. I wouldn't say we were hanging *out*. I just kind of met her, and she offered to cut my hair. It only took a few minutes."

"No boys?" Mom asked.

"What?"

"You weren't . . . *involved* with any boys?"

"Mom! No."

Not in the way she meant, anyway. I pictured Kylie Scarlet dogpaddling back to his clan and wondered how he'd redeem himself. Now that I was keeper I knew there were only two ways to lose our job: die or step down. Kylie would never step down—I felt certain of that. Sooner or later, I'd see him again. I might even be able to forgive him. What happened in the Hollow wasn't my fault, but I had kind of started it. Still, if Kylie thought he'd even things up by stealing *my* gold next time, he had another think coming.

Mom shook her head disapprovingly. "I don't like that Byron Berry. I've heard things about him, and I heard he was here. Did he give you those fireworks, Lily?"

"He didn't give me anything," I assured her, glad to be able to clear at least *his* reputation.

"You don't have to protect that boy."

"I'm not!"

Mom heaved a massive sigh. "Let me tell you what I think happened: You were mad at me for not staying home on your birthday. You were here by yourself, maybe a little bored, and Byron—or *someone*—gave you those fireworks, and you thought, 'Why not?' Except that you obviously didn't realize how dangerous fireworks are. You're lucky you still have both eyes!"

I nodded unhappily. That part, at least, was completely true.

"Some neighbors ran over, our window was broken, you found out I was on my way home, and you panicked. You bailed out your bedroom window to avoid facing the music. How am I doing?"

Not well. But letting her think what she wanted was better than having to lie.

I hung my head. "You make me sound like a bad kid."

Mom reached across the table and squeezed my hands.

"I don't think you're a bad kid, Lily. The thought of you wandering the streets all night terrifies me, and if you ever scare me like this again, I'll probably hurt you myself. . . . But we all make mistakes. You gave me plenty of time to reflect on mine."

Her tone gave me the courage to meet her eyes.

"I think you must believe I value work over you," she said.

"Well . . . *yeah*," I agreed sullenly.

"Lily, I need you to understand that you're the *reason* I work so hard. I don't like moving either, being so far from your gram and Aunt Sarah. I do it for you, for your future. You'll never be trapped by a job the way I am. I'm making sure you have options."

"You've never said you don't like moving before," I accused. "You always act like it's some big adventure."

"Because I wanted *you* to believe that. And that's another place I've failed. You aren't a little girl anymore. I can't just expect you to jump on board with whatever I decide. I'm going to explain things better, Lily, start talking them over with you. We're a team, you and I. There is no one and nothing more important to me than you."

"Really?"

"If something had happened to you last night and I hadn't gotten this chance to tell you how much I love you . . ." Mom broke off, in tears again.

I choked up right along with her. "I love you, too, Mom. I missed you so much."

"Okay, then." Rising from the table, she gathered me into her arms. "Let's just put this behind us and try to do better from here. I can do better, Lily." She laughed through her tears. "For one thing, you can be certain I'm taking your *next* birthday off!"

Mom stepped over to the counter. "I have birthday presents for you. We can open those later, but here's something special you'll want to see now."

She handed me a greeting card addressed in familiar green writing.

"Gigi!" I cried, ripping the envelope open.

"She must have left it with someone to mail for her, just in case she wasn't . . ." Mom shook her head. "It got here a day late, but it's pretty amazing it got here at all."

The front of the card depicted some artist's idea of a leprechaun sitting on a toadstool formed by the number thirteen. He was about two inches tall and wearing Louis XIV shoes with heels, striped stockings, puffy green shorts, and a gigantic clover boutonniere.

"Oh, that is so wrong," I said, flipping the card open.

Its printed message read, LUCKY YOU! YOU'RE 13! HAPPY BIRTHDAY!

And under that was a note from Gigi:

Happy Birthday, Lilybet!

I want you to know how proud I am
of you and of everything you've
accomplished. I may not be there in
person anymore, but you will always be the
keeper of my heart.

The only way back is forward!

Love you forever,

Gigi

"'The only way back is forward'?" Mom said, reading over my shoulder. "What's that supposed to mean?"

"Just . . . an inside joke," I said, sniffling.

Mom put her arm around my shoulders. "I've been too hard on your grandmother. I know she loved you, Lily. To plan that far ahead for a birthday card!"

"Yep. She was a keeper."

"And of course it *had* to be a leprechaun," Mom said, rolling her eyes.

"Um . . . huh?" I asked cautiously.

"I've never told you this before—and I don't mean it as an insult—but your Gigi was a bit barmy when it came to leprechauns. All those clovers she collected? Plus she used to say things sometimes, like, How could we be so sure that leprechauns weren't real? Where did we think all those stories about them came from? One time she actually

251

asked me, 'Maddy, if leprechauns *were* real, wouldn't they be fun to visit?'"

I felt a smile creep onto my face. Gigi certainly knew her way around a clover swear.

"It was all harmless fun, I guess, but I didn't want her filling your head with that nonsense—at least, not until you were old enough to know better. She promised she wouldn't, but I never knew. Your Gigi was a great one for getting her own way."

Mom shook her head, remembering. "I'll tell you what, though, Lily, I've never seen anything like that woman's luck."

I could only grin.

That night, alone in my bedroom, I sat and examined my keeper key. The familiar piece of gold was more precious to me now than ever, but I had found something even better: a way to go on loving Gigi without being sad anymore.

I would honor her memory by carrying on her secret legacy, and I'd do it with a happy heart, the way Gigi would have wanted.

"And someday," I whispered to the key, "I'm going to pass you down to a granddaughter of my own!"

Epilogue

O f course my mom made me go to gymnastics the next day, but I barely even minded. I walked into the gym in my green leotard and Horace Green footies ready for just about anything Ainsley Williams's clique could dish out.

"Lily!" Marti Gregory exclaimed, startled by my pixie into admitting she knew me. "Your hair!"

"Yeah, I cut it," I said. "It was getting too long."

"It's cute!"

I know. Giving her an empty smile, I took my usual place against the wall.

Ms. Carlson walked in, clapping. "All right, girls! Let's start stretching."

Ainsley, Jayce, and their four favorite cling-ons grabbed the mat front and center. All six of them were wearing pink or lavender leotards with matching eye shadow and barrettes. I sat twenty feet away and began stretching my straddle.

"What's up with the freak?" I heard Jayce ask the others. "She cut her hair or something."

They all turned to look. Instead of glancing away, like I normally did, I stared back in a make-my-day kind of way. Their voices dropped to whispers.

"Where was she yesterday?" Ainsley asked.

"I heard she blew up her front porch, then ran away," Darci James reported. "This guy I know, Byron, saw the whole thing."

"Freak!" Jayce said again, but her accompanying look of scorn held new caution. I could tell I'd just been elevated from weak and pathetic to unpredictable and possibly dangerous.

Perfect.

"We're going to work on roundoffs this morning," Ms. Carlson announced, "but we're going to try them on the beam. Who wants to demonstrate?"

Every hand in Team Ainsley shot into the air. Marti

caught my eye and shuddered, letting me know she'd be sitting this one out with me.

"All right, then. Ainsley," Ms. Carlson said. "Show us how it's done."

The whole class walked over to the balance beam. Ainsley hit the beatboard and sprang up onto the four-inch-wide surface, making her mount look easy.

"Roundoff on beam is just like on floor," Ms. Carlson told us, "except that your feet land toe to heel instead of side by side. Okay, Ainsley. Whenever you're ready . . ."

Ainsley's tight features betrayed her nervousness. She took a couple of steps down the beam, then turned a slow cartwheel, adjusting her hips at the last second to try to convert it into a roundoff. The balls of her feet spun precariously on four inches of wood . . . and kept on spinning. Her attempt ended in an ugly full-body wobble and a bail-out jump to the mat.

"Not bad," Ms. Carlson said as Ainsley skulked back to her friends. "Nice first try. Who wants to go—?"

Jayce's hand hit the air before the question was finished. Being friends in that group didn't mean they didn't live to show each other up—and while Ainsley was the group's queen, Jayce was the better gymnast.

"Jayce. All right," Ms. Carlson said.

Jayce did a scissors mount, then stalked down the

beam and pirouetted on its end, building up suspense with lots of showy shoulder shrugs and hand gestures. Finally, she got around to the actual roundoff. Her hands hit the beam fine, and so did her left foot, but her right foot missed completely and continued on through space. She didn't even have time for an Ainsley-style wobble before her free leg swung down, around, and back into the air, landing her butt-first in the crash pads beneath the beam.

"Nice," I said, applauding crisply. A few girls giggled behind their hands, secretly loving it as much as I did.

Ms. Carlson whipped around, intending to rip into the culprit. But finding out the culprit was me left her too surprised to speak.

"I suppose you think you could do better?" Jayce challenged angrily, struggling to her feet.

"I don't think I could do *worse.*"

"Let's see you, then." *Freak,* her lips added tauntingly.

"Well now . . ." Ms. Carlson had finally recovered her voice. "I'm not sure, Lily . . . maybe on the practice beam . . ."

But I already had a leg over the high beam. My feet swung onto the wood in front of me, and the next second I was standing up and hardly even shaking—at least, not until I looked down. Suddenly, calling Jayce's bluff didn't seem so smart anymore.

Maybe I wasn't feeling *this* lucky.

"You don't have to do this, Lily," Ms. Carlson said. "In fact, I think it will be better if you don't."

Jayce smirked. I stopped looking down.

"What's the worst thing that can happen?" I asked. "I land on my butt, right? We've already seen that demonstrated, and about as well as it can be done."

Louder giggles made the rounds. Even Ainsley smiled. Jayce's cheeks turned scarlet.

"Lily—" Ms. Carlson began.

I launched into my roundoff before she could say another word. Both my hands hit the beam square. *Just like a line on the mat,* I told myself as my hips twisted over my head. My feet came down together, one behind the other. My footies stuck to the wood. The next thing I knew, I was standing again, totally balanced and facing the opposite direction.

"Lily!" Marti squealed. "You did it!"

I stood motionless another few seconds, long enough for the entire class to be sure I had nailed it. Then I jumped down to the mat, landing right in front of Team Ainsley.

"My name is Lily," I said. "Start using it."

"Lily! Lily!" Kendall's voice carried across the parking lot, stopping me outside the shopping center on my way home from gymnastics. Her sandals slapped the asphalt as she ran up to meet me, a pink paper bag swinging from one arm. I had been dying to see her but hadn't dared call; I was still trying to think of a clover-swear-proof apology that would make Kendall sure to forgive me.

"Lily! What happened?" she demanded. "My mom said you were playing with fireworks, and your mom said you took off, and I was really worried about you!"

"Sorry," I mumbled, embarrassed. "And sorry about the other night too—standing you up and missing the movie and all. I didn't actually plan for any of that to happen."

"That's okay. I mean, *yeah,* but . . ." Kendall shook her head. "Are you all right?"

"I'm fine. It was just one of those stupid things that will never happen again." *At least, not so far as anyone human will know,* I added to myself.

We stood there, nodding awkwardly, not sure what to say. "What did you get?" I finally asked, pointing to Kendall's pink bag.

"This? No, I wasn't shopping. I brought this from home."

"Oh." We started walking together, moving through the parking lot in the general direction of Baskin-Robbins. "Are you getting ice cream?" I asked.

"Aren't you?"

"Not today. My mom said to go straight home and text her the second I get there."

Kendall grimaced sympathetically. "Is she pretty mad?"

"Not as mad as I thought she'd be. Still, I'd rather not be late."

"I didn't come for ice cream anyway. I was actually looking for you."

"Really?" I asked, amazed.

"Maybe we can hang out at your house today. If you want to," she added with an odd sideways glance of her blue eyes.

"Okay."

We crossed at the corner light and headed down the sidewalk toward our neighborhood. I still wasn't sure what was going on; I was just really glad that Kendall wasn't mad at me.

"Did you go see *Samurai Princess* with Lola?" I asked.

"Of course not. Listen, I was going to tell you this when we went out for your birthday, but—" Cutting herself off abruptly, Kendall dragged me under a shady tree and pulled a present out of her bag. "Here, this is for you. Happy birthday!"

"Kendall!" I exclaimed. "You didn't have to get me anything."

"I wanted to."

I hesitated two full seconds to admire the gift wrap. Then I started ripping. Underneath were a disposable camera and a photo album with pink fabric covers.

"I made that myself," she said, poking the album proudly. "Look. It's padded." Grabbing the camera, Kendall held it at arm's length and aimed for our heads. "Smile!"

A flash went off, leaving me blinking.

"There. That'll be your first picture. We can take more too. If you want." She had that weird look on her face again.

"Wait. Did you and Lola have a fight or something?"

"No, but that's what I wanted to tell you the other night. Me and Lola . . . She's a good friend and I'll still see her. But we aren't that alike anymore. I like hanging out with you now, Lily. I thought maybe we could hang out more."

"Really?" And then the best part hit me. "And you wanted to tell me this on my birthday?" That was *before* I'd come home with a new haircut, magic shoes, and a boatload of leprechaun luck. On my birthday, I'd been plain old Lily.

Kendall nodded. "So, do you want to? Be better friends, I mean."

I smiled as if I'd just been named keeper all over again. "Totally."

On the corner of our block, right as we made the turn, Kendall squealed and pointed. Byron Berry was coasting past my house, standing on his bike pedals to see in our front windows.

"Ooh, Lily!" Kendall teased. "I think someone likes you!"

I rolled my eyes as if she were crazy, but I walked a little taller. Who knew? Byron had never cruised my house *before.*

And then I noticed the rainbow. The arcing-out-of-a-clear-blue-sky-right-down-to-my-bedroom-roof rainbow. "Uh-oh. *That* doesn't happen in the Meadows."

"What?" Kendall said.

"Huh? Oh, just . . . mumbling."

I obviously needed to hide my gold better—and fast. *Underground,* I thought, instinctively guessing the solution. *That's where the leprechauns keep theirs.*

I needed to tell my mom about it too. And I would. Eventually. Definitely before college. Just as soon as I came up with a good story.

It will all work out, I thought with a secret smile. I was thirteen now and much better at dealing with things.

Besides, I was feeling lucky.

Laura Peyton Roberts is the author of many books for young readers, including the novels *Ghost of a Chance, The Queen of Second Place,* and *Queen B.* She lives with her husband in San Diego. Visit her at www.laurapeytonroberts.com.